LEVON'S KIN

CHUCK DIXON

LEVON'S KIN
Copyright © 2017 Chuck Dixon
All Rights Reserved
Editing, Cover and Interior by QA Productions
Cover Photo by Gavin Dixon
Battle cleaver courtesy of Waysun Johnny Tsai

BRUNO BOOKS

dixonverse.net

Other Works by Chuck Dixon

Levon Cade
Book 1: *Levon's Trade*
Book 2: *Levon's Night*
Book 2.5: *Levon's Ride*
Book 3: *Levon's Run*

BAD TIMES
Bad Times 1: Cannibal Gold
Bad Times 2: *Blood Red Tide*
Bad Times 3: *Avenging Angels*
Bad Times 4: *Helldorado*
Bad Times 5: *Sons of Heaven*

Gomers
Shrinkage
With John Morgan Neal: *Snakehand*

Seal Team Six: The Novel
Seal Team Six 2
Seal Team Six 3
Seal Team Six 4

Winterworld: The Mechanics Song
Batgirl/Robin Year One
Batman Versus Bane

1

The dogs were silent.

They usually started barking once they heard Kaylee walking up the gravel drive. The two dogs, a yappy poodle mix and a big yellow Lab, were still unheard even as the double-wide came in sight through the trees.

The pair of dogs were the reason Kaylee woke up before dawn every morning. She dressed in the dark and slipped silently from the trailer she and her mother shared. She'd be the only kid walking on the county road toward her school a mile away where the road crossed Branch Pike. The Pettits lived at the end of a long gravel drive halfway to school. Mr. Pettit was kind of scary with his arms and neck covered in tattoos. He had a nice smile though. Mrs. Pettit, "call me Tandy," was a sweet woman who dressed like a lady on one of those shopping channels on TV. Tandy told Kaylee to come by anytime she liked to play with the dogs.

"They do look forward to it," she assured Kaylee. Mr. Pettit grunted in agreement, allowing that the pair of dogs did enjoy the time Kaylee spent with them each day.

Kaylee dearly desired to own a dog of her own, a dog she could hug and love and give a name of her own choosing. But her mother complained that dogs were too much work even though Kaylee's mother did little else but spend days in the trailer, smoking and watching television.

She crunched over the gravel past the pair of carports. Mr. Pettit's bass boat and his motorcycle were under one with tarps thrown over them. Tandy's Camaro, polished to a mirror shine, rested under the other. Mr. Pettit's big pickup squatted on fat tires on the turnaround before the front entrance of the double-wide.

The truck shone like glass in the streaks of liquid shimmers coming through the birches. The siding on the double-wide was spotted with yellow mold. The white shingles of the roof were streaked with black. A window at the front had been repaired with duct tape now all puckered at the edges.

The screen door lay partly open. It was crooked on a busted hinge. The house door was open as well. Kaylee stood at the foot of the wooden deck and squinted into the gloom within the house.

"Peanut? Honey?" she whispered.

There was no frantic scrabble of claws on tile. No eager yelps. The dark beyond the open doorway was undisturbed.

She stepped to the deck, repeating the names of the poodle and Lab. Braced in the doorway, she allowed a moment for her eyes to adjust to the deeper dimness inside the house. A humped figure lay on the tile of the family room. A smaller heap was nearby. Kaylee took a cautious step inside the house, wincing as her sneakered foot caused the floorboards to creak.

Honey, the big dopey, friendly Labrador, lay on her side in a black pool. Peanut, the little poodle, was unmoving at the edge of the lake. Dark boot prints were spotted over the linoleum from someone who stepped into the black spill toward the bedrooms at the back of the house. Kaylee looked down at her own feet to see she stood atop sticky boot prints. Turning, she saw fainter prints beneath the dew of condensation on the boards of the deck. The departing steps of someone who had left the house not long ago.

Her breath held tight in her lungs, Kaylee moved deeper into the house. She skirted along the walls, avoiding the dark boot prints.

Her voice soft, she called for the Pettits. The answer was a silence greater than the absence of sound. The silence was a thing apart, as if the air was occupied by an alien element altering the atmosphere within the house.

At the door to the main bedroom, Kaylee stopped and placed her hands on the doorframe to steady herself. The Pettits lay side by side on the king-sized bed that dominated the room. They lay flat on their backs, fully dressed but for shoes. Their hands were joined between them. They might have been sleeping peacefully. Or perhaps lying together under an open sky to gaze upward at the stars.

Except the mattress under them was stained a deep crimson. And their heads, sightless and staring, sat atop Mrs. Pettit's vanity table.

Kaylee's scream rose to a piercing tone startling to flight a herd of whitetails grazing on shoots a mile from the Pettit house.

Gunny Leffertz said:

"Nothing harder than leaving home except for going home."

2

They drove down the two-lane through woods crowding in either side of the curving road. The bare branches of trees created a cathedral above them. Sunlight flashed on snow still clinging in the hollows. The road followed the high valley along a path of least resistance. It dropped down into the shadowed bellies of divides dark and cold. It drifted along ridgelines where the land dropped away to reveal waves of forested hills rolling toward the horizon.

Levon piloted a Toyota SUV bearing Arkansas plates with the ease of a man on a road well-traveled in the past. Each new turn and landmark recalled moments from a history so long ago it seemed like the memory of a stranger.

In the seat beside him, Merry, his daughter, stirred from her own thoughts.

"Will they like me?" she said.

"Who's that, honey?" he said.

"Your family."

"They're your family too, Merry."

"I never met them. I never even knew about them."

"That's going to change starting today."

"But will they like me?"

"They'll love you."

Out the window she could see homes nestled in the woods at the ends of driveways. The trees gave way to more homes along either side of the road. They paused at a four-way stop. Around the intersection was a gas station with a food mart, a car repair place, a brick building with a flag out front, and an ice cream stand with a marquee sign announcing it was CL SED TIL SUM ER. The only sign of life was a man pumping gas into an ATV on a trailer behind a primer-shot pickup.

They left the crossing behind. The houses thinned out again. The woods closed in once more.

"Are we almost to Uncle Fern's?" Merry asked.

"Almost," Levon said.

"You said it was just past Colby."

"That's Colby we just drove through."

"That was a town? A gas station and an ice cream place?"

"Out here that is a town, honey."

"Where's the nearest *real* town?"

"You mean with a Walmart?" he said.

"Yeah," she said, nodding.

"That would be Haley down off the state road. It's about an hour away from where we'll be."

"Is there a Wendy's there?"

"It's been a long time since I've been there. Might be a Wendy's there by now. We'll ride down after we're settled at Uncle Fern's."

Merry sat watching the woods go by, imagining the animals living there just out of sight in the shadows between the trees.

"I can't believe you really have an Uncle Fern," she said after a bit.

"I tell you about him all the time."

"I thought he was made up. Like Santa Claus or the Easter Bunny."

"He's real all right. He's your uncle, too, honey. Your great uncle. My dad's brother."

"What kind of name is Fern?"

"A made-up name. Like a nickname. Uncle Fern's real name is George Martin Cade."

"Then why's he called Fern?"

"Just something people do around here. For some reason they started calling him Fern and it stuck."

"They come up with a made-up name for you, Daddy?"

"Nope. I was always just Levon."

The road divided ahead into a 'Y' fork with a surface of rutted asphalt veering away to the right. Levon turned onto the broken road. A shelf of white-washed wood formed a rest for a row of steel mailboxes, seven in all. A faded wooden plaque at the fork sign promised local honey and free-range eggs in neat hand-painted letters. The busted road surface gave way to a rutted lane of packed gravel that climbed along the base of a hill. Other lanes came off the road either side. Merry saw some rooftops way out in the trees. Satellite dishes perched atop the ridge lines. She could smell wood smoke coming from somewhere.

Levon turned the wheel to take them onto a dirt track nearly invisible in the brush along the shoulder. Branches scraped along the sides of the Toyota before the bushes opened up into the white boles of beeches. After a while the road went level and the trees thinned out. A farmhouse with wood siding and a deep, screened porch sat at the edge of a clearing. A steel frame barn and a carport were set either side in a sort of courtyard. Some kind of car was under a pile of tarps under the carport. A carefully preserved International Harvester pickup was parked on the crushed gravel lot before the house.

The screen door of the porch banged open. Dogs raced over the ground toward the Toyota. Three redbone hounds baying and leaping. And a ridgeback with mottled fur barked, head ducking, as it trotted around the strange car.

A man marched from the house in their wake. He moved with

a limp, swinging one leg wide. A big man with hunched shoulders and a paunch pushing out the bib of his overalls. White Elvis sideburns streaked yellow, a white bristle of hair under a crushed Ford ball cap. He whistled once then growled wordless commands, waving his hands to part the howling dogs. They shushed and milled about his legs as he neared the car. The ridgeback slumped away across the yard toward the barn.

"Levon?" the man said, eyes narrowed.

Levon stood by the open door of the Toyota, allowing his uncle to study him.

"It's me, Uncle Fern," he said.

"And your little girl?" Fern said. He leaned forward, peering through the sunlight reflection on the windshield.

"The dogs have her spooked."

"Get her on out here. Those dumb hounds won't hurt her unless she's a raccoon. You aren't a raccoon, are you, honey?"

Merry stepped out on the driver's side to stand close by her father. The hounds trotted around to sniff at her legs and hands. The ridgeback kept its distance, blue eyes fixed on Levon.

"Damn. She's a pretty one, nephew. A miracle on a level with the loaves and fishes given how ugly your pan is," Fern said, smiling at her.

"Thank you, sir," Merry said low, eyes to the heads of the dogs bobbing around her.

"The dogs like you so I guess you're okay. I got some chili on the stove for lunch. I can always open another can. Come in and have a bowl," Fern said. He turned to hobble back to the house. Merry followed with the hounds in a train behind her.

Levon raised the hatch and pulled a pair of duffels from the cargo area of the Toyota. He watched Uncle Fern hold the door for Merry, both already chatting away. He pulled up his jacket to remove the Colt automatic from his waistband. He unzipped one of the duffels and dropped the handgun atop the bundles of cash heaped inside. The absence of the weight of it left him feeling light. Levon raised his head and closed his eyes. It felt like a hundred years since he'd done that. He took a deep pull of the cool air through his nostrils. The scent of old timber and woodland funk filled his nostrils. The woods were waking up as the days grew longer. Green sprouts on the tips of the beech limbs. The tang of chili followed along with the smoke from the farm house's chimney. An aftertaste of machine oil from the low shape under a tarp inside the carport.

He opened his eyes to scan the world around him. Beyond the humble buildings the forest spread uphill and down in every direction creating a silent curtain that closed the world out to all but what he could see fifty yards in any direction. In his mind he could see well past the trees to deer trails, springs, washes, promontories and creeks that made up the landscape for miles around. They would be unchanged. They would be as he left them, as he remembered them growing up in these hills and deeps.

Levon Cade was home.

3

Their shifts overlapped so they met at Carmine's for dinner.

Nancy Valdez dipped the end of a breadstick into a pool of marinara at the edge of Bill's plate.

"I thought you were watching your carbs," Bill Marquez said, pointing at her salad with a forkful of penne pasta.

"I'll take a run after work. Besides, now we'll both smell like garlic," she said, shrugging.

"But not to each other."

"Exactly."

He smiled across the table at her. She returned her attention to her salad. He wasn't happy to be out of the field but he was happy to be assigned to the DC office. For the time being. It allowed him to get to know Nancy better. He spent a couple nights a week at her place. She spent a few nights at his room at the Marriott Residence in Alexandria. Being stationed in Washington was the Big Show for most Bureau agents. But Bill knew it was purely temporary for him. The Bureau let him know by putting him up at the Marriott the past month and a half. In any case his desk was a ten minute cab ride from Nancy's office at Treasury. For now, things were good.

"How's the task force?" she asked.

"Down to a force of one."

"Shit." She put down her fork and raised her eyes to his.

"They sent Piniella back to Dallas and Morgan got orders to join an investigation in Buffalo."

"You're alone on this?"

"Even my assistant got reassigned. Carol? The gum chewer?"

"So they're closing you out?" she said.

"I figure a week or more and they'll pull me away to something else," he said, stirring his penne. "You know how it is. New shit hits the fan every day. We're undermanned."

"It's the same at Treasury. We wanted this guy, too, but the feebs hogged lead on it so . . ."

"Well, Levon Cade has lost his glow. He's not as sexy as domestic ISIS operatives."

"He's probably ten thousand miles away by now. He's had weeks to fly and all the money to run on."

Bill put his fork down, his appetite evaporated.

"All I have is a name and a background history that is pure bullshit. He was born. He got a GED. He joined the Marines. He was married. His wife died of cancer. He has a little girl. The rest is so loaded with redactions they should have printed it on black paper."

"Someone's covering for him," Nancy said. She reached across the table to brush the back of his hand with her fingers.

Bill sighed.

"*Everybody's* covering for him. That Fenton woman up in Maine won't give me jack. If I ask her what time it is she stops to think about it. She can't remember one thing about a guy who was her neighbor for almost a year. I can't blame her. It looks like this Cade saved her and her kids from being butchered."

"And the Marine sergeant? Mississippi, was it?"

"The gunny. He won't give up anything. I *know* his wife took the Cade kid off the train in Memphis. I *know* the kid stayed at his cabin. Probably Cade too. I *know* that old jarhead hid them out. But he won't give. His wife either. They're stone silent on the subject of Levon Cade. And I have zero leverage."

"You need to lean on them by other means."

"Threaten them with audits? Take away benefits? A woman grateful to the man who saved her children? An old, black Marine vet? Old, black, *blind* Marine vet? I'm not that kind of Fed."

"Treasury would do it if they were lead. We'd be up to our ass in their financials." Nancy poked at her salad to spear an olive.

"It's all financials to you. This Cade might hold the key to billions in untaxed funds. He's a mile-high dollar sign."

"Possibly, Bill. He left Maine with more than cash. I *feel* it."

"To the Bureau he's a possible terror threat. He checks all the boxes. That's the only way I've kept the investigation alive *this* long."

"You think he's linked to homegrown terror?"

"No. I'm not sure what he is but he's not that."

"You'll find an angle on him," she said.

"I'd better find it soon," he said.

"I still say he's in Thailand by now."

"No," Bill said with conviction. "He's still here somewhere. He ran but he's the kind of guy who only runs so long and so far."

"The daughter?" Nancy said.

"Yeah. She might be the key."

It was his turn to pick up the check. He walked her to the curb and they shared a garlicky kiss before she stepped into a cab. He walked to where he left his Bureau car in the alley behind Carmine's. Illegal as hell but the plaque on the dash kept the tickets away.

On the drive back through beep and creep evening traffic he thought about what Nancy said and what he answered.

Meredith Cade.

It *was* all about the little girl.

4

"You have a lot of books, Uncle Fern. Daddy's other friend has a lot of books, too," Merry said returning to the kitchen after her tour of the house. The dogs paced behind her, nails tapping on the plank floor.

"There's no end to learning, girl," Fern said, setting two mugs of hot coffee on the table while Levon carried the empty chili bowls to the steel sink.

"Who's Mickey Spillane?" she said.

"Only the greatest writer who ever lived," Fern said.

"He only says that because Spillane was a Marine, too," Levon said from where he ran water in the bowls.

"You were a Marine like Daddy?"

"Damn straight," Fern said. He rolled up the cuff of his flannel shirt to show Merry a tattoo of a snarling bulldog wearing a drill instructor's campaign hat. The letters USMC were in bold beneath the dog.

"A long time ago, right?" Merry said, eyes on the fading ink.

"Busted my cherry over Tet. Three tours in 'Nam. And Marine tours were—"

"Thirteen months," Levon finished for him.

"Smartass," Fern said, pouring a dollop of honey into his coffee.

"Why don't you unpack your things, honey? Fix your room the way you like?" Levon said. He joined Fern at the table.

"My room? Which room?" she said.

"Take the one at the corner back. It's got the prettiest view come spring. 'Nother month and all you'll see is dogwood blossoms out the windows," Fern said.

Merry took off running, the dogs close behind. Sneakered feet and paws charged up the stairs, resounding through the house.

Fern regarded Levon through the steam rising off the dark liquid in the mug raised to his lips.

"What kind of trouble are you in?"

"Can't a man come home and visit family?"

"Don't shit a shitter, nephew. You haven't been back here since before you were shaving regular. Now it's old home week? Tell me straight or stop drinking my coffee."

"I have the law looking for me. Merry, too."

"What kind of law?"

"What kind you got? All of them, I guess. I can pay my way."

"You're gonna make me get up off this chair and kick your ass."

"I only want you to know I have money."

"Your money?"

"Mine now. Nobody's looking for it."

"I might know the reason why. So the law wants your ass not your money."

"It's not so simple."

"Never is, nephew."

They sipped coffee, strong and sweet, in silence for a while. They could hear shuffling feet and pattering paws from the floor above.

"You stay as long as you like or as long as you need to," Uncle Fern said at last.

Levon nodded then frowned, eyes cast to the table.

"Something wrong with that?" Fern said.

"We'll stay. But only if I make the coffee from now on," Levon said.

* * *

The floor was barn planks worn bare of varnish at the center of the room. A simple iron frame bed and chipped white dresser were the only furnishings. The walls had faded squares on the plaster where pictures once hung. Merry found sheets, pillows and covers for the bed on a shelf in the closet. She made the bed, shooing the hounds away from climbing atop it. They made a game of it until she chased them from the room and closed the door behind them.

The three hounds were named Woody, Tobey and Tex. She only ever heard her uncle call the ridgeback 'feller' but wasn't sure of the dog's name or if it even had a name. Feller kept to himself, not a part of the mini-pack formed by the three hounds. He kept close to Uncle Fern mostly and always seemed to be somewhere nearby where he could silently watch over the man.

A rolled carpet leaned in a corner of the room. Merry worked the twine from it and laid it out to cover the bare section of floor. The rug was made of intertwined rags to make up a pattern of diamond shapes in white and blue. The white portion was yellowed in spots but the rug smelled clean. It made the room seem friendlier, less empty.

She unpacked the big duffel of her clothes; all new from a K-mart they passed back in Corinth on the way to Uncle Fern's. The store was closing so they were able to load up on jeans, socks, t-shirts, panties and two new pairs of sneakers at discount prices. Merry stripped the tags and stickers off. She folded the items and placed them in the drawers. There were a few new paperback books as well. Those she lined up atop the dresser. She hadn't seen a television anywhere in the house so expected to do a lot of reading. She'd check out some Mickey Spillane when she was done with the books she brought. Maybe Colby had a library.

From a side pocket of the duffel she pulled the little stuffed gorilla her father had given her. Back in Baltimore, was it? She put it by the books.

The empty duffel stowed under the bed, she lay back on the crisp sheets and watched shadows play across the ceiling by light cast through the windows along two walls of the room. The bare limbs outside the windows made shifting patterns across the cracked plaster. She rolled onto her belly and looked at the walls opposite the windows. The empty squares where pictures once hung. She wondered who might have been in the pictures and why Uncle Fern took them down. Maybe whoever once slept in this room took the pictures when they left.

Merry wished she had pictures to put in their place. Of her mother. Of her father, younger, in his blue uniform and hair cut almost bald. Herself as a baby, smiling goofy with little pink clips in her wispy hair. Those pictures were gone now. In the past. Left behind when they left Huntsville. She'd never see them again. There was too much distance between who she was then and who she was now.

Her father called from the foot of the stairs.

"Merry. Come on down here."

She lay still for a moment smiling.

Merry.

She could have her own name again.

Merry Cade launched herself from the bed and raced from the room, startling the dogs lying outside the door to await her.

Gunny Leffertz said:
> *"Everything in this world is always changing. Except people. People don't know how to change. Or don't want to."*

5

Haley was a town with two faces. To one side of the interstate and two miles east, the old town sat nestled in trees at the bottom of a broad valley. The old town was mostly boarded up storefronts, a Citgo station and a Legion hall. Four blocks deep either side of Main Street lay old two-bedroom bungalows once occupied by mill workers. The textile mill was closed, torn down years before. An empty lot that served as a weekend flea market was all that was left to mark the spot. The flea was the only going concern in town.

To the other side of the interstate was a golden mile of fast food places, strip malls, a Home Depot and a Walmart. The stores there, built in the '90s and later, served the people living in subdivisions, developments and trailer parks that took root in a ten mile radius around the cloverleaf where the state road met the raised concrete surface of the interstate. The lower house prices made up for the long commute up to Huntsville or down to Birmingham.

Levon piloted a cart along the aisles of the Winn-Dixie while Merry hunted for the stuff on the list Uncle Fern gave them.

"We'll do frozen last," Levon said.

"We might need another cart," Merry said. She tumbled an armload of cellophane wrapped sandwich cookies on top of the load. The basket was full near to the top and the lower shelf was loaded as well.

"You go on. I'll grab us another one," he said.

At the front he freed a new cart from a long row and turned to reenter the store.

"Goose?"

A broad-shouldered man was entering through the automatic doors. The same height as Levon. Dirty blond hair going thin on top and worn long at the back. Thick wrists and rough hands visible below the cuffs of a canvas farmer's coat. Lower lip abulge with chew. A quart-sized soda cup in his hand.

"That you, Goose?" The man stepped closer, head bent to study Levon's face with an inquisitive eye.

"Hey, Dale," Levon said, bringing his cart to a stop in front of the newspaper rack.

"Never thought I'd see you back in the county, brother." A juicy grin creased his face around the chew. His eyes flashed with a glint of amusement.

"Well, here I am."

"Heard your wife died. She was pretty. I never met her. Somebody showed me a picture."

"That was a few years back."

"You visiting? You ain't here to stay, are you? Be like back in the day if you're home for good."

"Not in such a rush to relive those days, Dale," Levon said. His hands were fists on the cart handle.

"Some things best left as they are. You know what I mean?" The glint turned to sadness in Dale's eyes.

Merry pushed the cart to the front of the pet food aisle and stopped to look for her father. The cart was full with no room for the sacks of dog chow on Uncle Fern's list. She spotted her father on the other side of the checkouts. He was talking to someone. A man who was standing close to her father and gesturing with a hand as he spoke. She didn't like the man. Something about his face. Something about the way he was talking to her father.

Merry left the cart to join her father. She stopped by a conveyor when the man put a hand to her father's arm and gripped it. Levon pulled away, breaking free. Her father pushed the cart away on an empty aisle between two closed registers. The man remained standing where he was, eyes on Levon. He watched awhile, brows lowered, before spitting into a soda cup then turning to leave the store.

She waited until the man was out of sight to rejoin her father. Her sneakers squeaked on the tiles as she worked to heave the loaded cart forward.

"Who was he?" she asked.

"Someone I used to know back when I was growing up," Levon said. He switched carts with her, taking the loaded cart and parking it in place before an endcap.

"You're friends?" Merry already knew the answer. Nothing about anything she saw made her think her father and the other man were ever close friends.

"Just someone I used to know. What kind of kibble is it those dogs like?"

"Store brand. Uncle Fern says they're not picky."

Levon hefted two forty-pound bags into the cart.

"Last thing to get is the frozen stuff," Merry said.

He steered the cart into the next aisle with Merry following.

They stopped at a Wendy's across the lot from a Walgreen's.

"That order will hold us a while," Levon said. He took a pull of a soda.

"Until Uncle Fern runs out of cookies," Merry said. She dumped her fries onto her sandwich wrapper.

The SUV was pulled up to a spot where they could see it from their booth. The contents of two brimming carts were stowed in the rear of the Toyota. The frozen goods down under two big bags of ice.

"He's always had a sweet tooth. They called him Sugar when he was a kid. I think my daddy gave him that one."

"You said they called him Fern."

"No. Fern he picked up when he was in the Corps. They started calling him that in Vietnam. I never asked why. You shouldn't either."

"I know. Mom taught me. Never ask soldiers about the past."

"Fern wasn't a soldier, honey. He was a Marine."

"What's the difference?"

"That's kind of hard to put into words a little girl might understand."

Merry crunched away at her chicken sandwich, eyes on him watching the Toyota. She took a sip of soda to wash it down.

"Does it take bad words to explain the difference between a soldier and a Marine?" she said.

He took his eyes off the car to smile at her. An actual genuine open smile from her father. It was a rare sight and made her blink.

"Not bad words, Merry. Just hard words."

"Big words? I know a lot of big words."

"No. Not big words."

She took another bite and tilted her head at him.

"All right. Listen up. But no more questions for today," he said.

She swallowed and leaned forward, eyes fixed on him.

"Soldiers are trained to fight. Marines are trained to kill."

"Isn't it the same thing?"

"No, it's not. It's a big difference. See, when an enemy sees it's the Army coming they know it's war. When they see Marines coming they know it's the end. Can you understand?"

"I think so." She chewed the end of her straw. Her eyes darted to him.

Levon raised a finger, a trace of a smile on his lips.

"No more questions for today."

She nodded assent.

But tomorrow was another day.

Gunny Leffertz said:
"Trouble never knocks. It just walks on in."

6

Next morning, Fern found Levon regrouting tile in the house's only bathroom.

"Gonna have to piss in the woods, old man," Levon said.

"It's raining, thank you kindly."

Levon shrugged.

"You don't need to do this, nephew."

"My daughter's going to be using this head. I'd like to at least bring it up to code." Levon finished a line of grout and lifted the gun clear. He ran a wet finger between two tiles to smooth the strand.

"That why you bought all this shit at the Home Depot?" Fern leaned in the doorway with a sour look.

"I'd like to stay busy while I'm here. God know this shack needs it."

"I got tools."

"When you can find them."

Fern snorted.

"Your little girl's locked the dogs out the house. She's mopping the kitchen floor. You'd think I lived like a pig."

"She likes to be busy too. Let her play house. It can't hurt anything to square away things for you." Levon stood and inspected the floor, the new grout gleaming white. He wrapped a wad of toilet paper around the end of the tube secured in the grout gun.

"And what do I owe you for the chow?" Fern said. He watched Levon sweep curled strings of ancient grout into a dustpan.

"Consider it our first month's board."

"I didn't ask you to do this."

Levon stood and leaned back on the basin cabinet. He took a breath and let it out.

"We're going to be here a while, Fern. It's an imposition on a cranky old loner like you. We'd like to pay our own way. It's only fair."

"I don't . . ." Uncle Fern said, lowering his head.

"I need to ask you something. I don't mean to embarrass you but I have to know."

Fern looked up, eyes ablaze.

"How you making ends meet?" Levon said.

"My veteran's check. Last year I sold some timber off the hill. That's all." Fern's eyes were narrowed, the pupils dark.

"No extra income? No thumpers hidden away somewhere?"

"A long while back maybe. It ain't like that around here no more. Nothing's the same as when you left."

"Because we can't be anywhere where there's law might be sniffing around."

"They have no reason to be looking here. Not for a long time. There hasn't been a thumper working in these woods since '98. Hell, Drew Miller went legit with his brand. Has a licensed outfit working in the old A&P market down in Haley." Fern smirked, still struck by the wonder of it.

"Okay. I had to ask," Levon said. He pushed off the basin cabinet and stooped to pick up his new tool box.

"It's all right. How about chicken tonight?" Fern said. He moved to allow Levon past him.

Both men were surprised to find Merry had materialized by them, a mop in her hand.

"What's a thumper?"

* * *

After lunch Levon took her to see the still.

He led her down the hill behind the barn and into the woods beyond. The hounds joined them, running ahead, noses snuffling through leaves wet from a shower that morning. All but Feller who stayed in his place under the kitchen table while Uncle Fern cleared the lunch dishes from the table. The boles of the trees were still stained black from the downpour. All around them they could hear the patter of drops coming down off the high branches.

The way ahead was invisible to Merry but her father made his way along a winding deer trail as sure as someone else walking the sidewalk of a familiar street. The woods closed in around them to create a stifling quiet broken only by her tramping feet. Her father walked quieter. Despite his size he moved with a near noiseless gait. His head did not turn but she saw his eyes were always in motion, sweeping the shadows around them for movement.

They followed a fold in the ground that dropped into a high walled cleft; a tangle of tree roots formed the walls either side. At the foot of the fold was a clearing in the trees carpeted with broad-leafed ferns. At the edge of the ferns stood a wooden shack the size of a single car garage. Its plank roof had partly collapsed over time. A rusted stove pipe leaned crookedly against a bare roof joist. A stack of split firewood was piled against one wall of the shed. It was covered in clumps of moss. A rusted lawn chair, its legs bent, crouched in the weeds.

Levon led the way around to the opening of the three-sided shelter. Merry followed, eyes on the ground to step around the litter of plastic gallon jugs and buckets lying everywhere under the ferns. The hounds milled about, snuffling in the ferns.

A fat copper tank, corroded green with age, sat in the center of the shed. Loops of metal tubing drooped down the side. There was a lingering scent of something spoiled in the air. Back in the shadowed interior a stack of cardboard cartons surrendered to rot. More plastic jugs were spilled from them.

"Uncle Fern made moonshine here?" Merry said.

"No one calls it moonshine. We called it whiskey or white or juice," Levon said.

"Did you use to make it?"

"I helped. Cut wood. Fetched water. Made a few deliveries for Fern and my dad."

"So it was like a family business?" Merry said. She was inside the shed squinting at a calendar from a car dealership in Birmingham. The calendar was fifteen years old.

"Better step out of there. No telling when this old shack might fall in." He touched her arm. She stepped back into the dappled sunlight.

"Your daddy's gone, right?"

"A lotta years now. Died right after I went into the Marines. Cancer."

"Like my mom."

"Different kind of cancer. But yeah."

Merry listened to the sounds of the woods. The chirrup of birds. The knocking of a woodpecker somewhere. The hounds were quiet now, lying panting in a group, eyes on her and Levon.

"Why do you call it a thumper?" she said.

"Because when the mash reaches a boil the steam rises into the curly tube at the top of the tank. The pressure of all the heated air makes a thumping noise. Like a drum."

"The mash is what you make the moon—whiskey out of?"

"Yeah. A mix of almost anything that'll rot. Apple peels. Potatoes. Sorghum. Even cattle feed. Your uncle knows a man in the next county used dandelions."

"That's what I smell? Rotten fruit and stuff?"

"It clings to the wood. Smells worse when it's cooking. Worst of all is a batch my dad made out of watermelon rinds. Smelled like sweet pickles. I went to school with my clothes stinking. My mom couldn't wash it out."

Merry knew a little about her grandmother. She knew she died in a bus accident years before. Her father told her his mom was on the way to a church event in the next state when a semi crossed the highway median.

"What's it taste like? Does it taste like apples? Or pickles?" she said.

"Always tasted the same to me. Plain awful. Burned like gasoline."

"Then why does anyone drink it?"

"To get drunk, I guess."

"Why do they want to be drunk?"

"Right there, little girl, is a question for the ages."

Levon took her by the hand to turn her from the shed. They started back the way they came. The hounds roused themselves to trot after.

It was spitting rain again when they reached the crest of the hill. Levon pulled Merry against him under the shelter of his farm coat. They walked on at an awkward pace. She trying to match his stride with long steps, he taking halting steps to throw off her pace and making her giggle. As they came in sight of the smoke curling from the chimney, Merry felt her father's hand tighten its grip on her shoulder.

A pickup truck with big knobby tires was pulling up on the gravel before the house.

On the doors of the crew cab was the county emblem for the sheriff's department. The truck came to a stop and a man in a police uniform got out.

It was the same man Merry saw talking to her daddy at the Winn-Dixie the day before.

7

"Hey, Goose," Dale said and stepped from the truck at Levon's approach.

"Go on inside, honey," Levon said.

Merry ducked from under the tent of her father's coat and ran through the pelting rain for the porch. Uncle Fern stepped from the screen door, his eyes on the men in his yard. Feller brushed past to stand at the edge of the porch, glowering through the railings.

"Can we talk where it's dry?" Dale said.

"This way," Levon said and walked to the carport. Dale followed.

They stood either side of the tarp-covered car. The rain rang off the sheet steel roof above them. Dale took off his Smokey hat and laid it atop the hood.

"This the old Mustang?" Dale said. He lifted a corner of a tarp revealing a primer coated fender. The wheels were off. The car rested atop jack stands and concrete blocks.

"Yeah."

"Man, she was fast. Shit on turns though. Fishtailed like a son-bitch unless she had a load of white in the trunk."

Levon said nothing.

"Your uncle's a sentimental one, keeping this here for you all this time. Not like you. Staying away all this time."

"What's your deal, Dale?"

"Only didn't want to leave things like they were at the Dixie. Me knowing you were back. Me being with the county now."

"You telling me how it's going to be?"

"I come here friendly." Dale parted his shiny nylon uniform jacket to show he wore no gun belt.

"Still have your badge," Levon said.

Dale sighed. He fished in a jacket pocket and came up with pack of cigarettes. He poked one out and got it started with a lighter fished from another pocket.

"There's all kinds of shit about you in alerts and shit. And your little girl. BOLOs and APBs and Homeland Security. I'd even believe some of it if you'd changed your name to Abdul or Mohammed or some shit."

"I got in some trouble. I'm working my way out of it."

"And you came home because you're safe here. Safe so long as no law knows you're here."

Levon said nothing.

"Well, you know about that as well as I do, Goose. There's what's the law and then there's what's right. And in this county that's all up to how a man sees the world."

"And how do you see it, Dale?"

Dale took a long drag on the Pall Mall. He filled his lungs before blowing a blue stream out toward the sheet of water rolling off the roof.

"We've known each other forever. Been in every kind of trouble together. I left right after you. Joined the Army. Broke my hip and my leg falling off a truck near Tikrit. Came back here and took the police tests. Was even married for five minutes to a girl from Haley."

"You're getting to a point here?" Levon said.

"I know you. I know the man you are. And I'm saying you got no worries from my end. Far as I'm concerned you're long dead or long gone or both and I ain't seen you."

"And the rest of the deputies?"

"They don't know you. They never leave the county roads.

Never come back up these switchbacks. You maintain the legal speed limit and you'll never meet up with one unless it's at Fay's." The donut shop in Colby.

"How hard are they looking for me?"

"Nobody in the county's looking for you anywhere."

"The Feds."

"They eased up about a month back. But they were hot and heavy for you for a while. They got you on all their shit lists and I see your name and picture now and then along with all the other swinging dicks they can't catch."

Levon leaned both hands on the hood of the Mustang and studied Dale's face.

"So, we straight on this, Goose?" Dale said. He let the last lungful of smoke from his mouth and crushed the butt out on the tarp.

"As long as you don't call me that around my little girl," Levon said.

Merry stood on the porch and watched her father and the man in the uniform come around the front of the car and shake hands. The sheriff's deputy clapped a hand to her father's shoulder. They stood a bit, talking easy in front of the car. The deputy gesturing with his hands as he spoke. Her father nodding as he sat hip-shot on a fender of the covered car. Merry wasn't sure, because of the driving rain between them, but she thought she might have seen her father smile.

"Are they friends?" she said.

"They're brothers," Uncle Fern said before turning to reenter the house.

The ridgeback trotted after, leaving Merry to stare in wonder at the two men talking in the rain.

8

"They're shutting us down Friday. The case is still officially open but only on paper. Cade goes on the back burner," Bill Marquez said.

"What about you?" Nancy Valdez said.

They decided to take a walk after a Chinese dinner in Georgetown. Arm in arm they strolled along storefronts with the tourists.

"Minneapolis. Playing catch up on some Syrian refugees settled there. Background checks."

"At least you'll be there in summer."

"Yeah." He shrugged.

"And in the field. They did *that* for you anyway. Got you out of the office," she said.

"I had the option to stay in Washington. Well, Quantico."

"But you don't want to."

"I considered it."

"Why would you? You don't want to be an instructor. You're too young."

He gave her arm a squeeze and she turned to him. Bill wore a silly apologetic smile.

"Oh no," she said. "Don't put that on me."

"I'm going to miss this. I like being around you. You like it, too."

"After two weeks of breathing canned air in a classroom and fighting Beltway traffic you'd hate me."

"Not possible," he said. Bill released her arm and turned her on the sidewalk to face him. He drew her with him under the green awning of a book store. The yellow light from inside highlighted her green eyes. They were beautiful despite the cast of suspicion in them.

"Please don't tell me you're about to get serious," she said. A mild scolding tone in her voice.

"All I'm saying is, Treasury is still going to want this guy. He still has a high dollar value on him," he said.

"Well, with the Bureau going cold on him we'll probably be amping up on our end. With you clowns out of the way we can grind away at getting closer."

"Any hits recently?"

"A bill from the Maine score showed up in Franklin, Tennessee. Another in Jonesboro, Arkansas. We need another half dozen for a pattern to start triangulating. I still think Cade's a million miles away."

"And I still think you're wrong. But you have the best shot of tracking him down and bringing the Bureau back into this."

"You're saying?"

"Get a twenty on this asshole and we get to spend some more time together," Bill said.

"That might just be the most romantic thing anyone's ever said to me," Nancy said. She was shaking her head at him but smiling all the same.

9

Merry woke to sounds from downstairs. A high keening whine and the voices of first her uncle and then her father. They were shouting over the howling of a dog. The light through her windows was gray when she opened her eyes.

She ran barefoot down the stairs. Her father was kneeling on the linoleum in the kitchen, stroking the flanks of one of the hounds. The dog was whimpering and yelping, his ribs bellowing with rapid breaths. Uncle Fern was on the phone speaking to someone. The ridgeback lay under the kitchen table bearing witness.

"What happened to Tex?" she said. Her voice caught when she saw the smears of blood on the tiles leading to the dog door.

"He ran into a porcupine," Levon said. He had the hound's collar tight in his fist while he ran gentle fingers along the dog's side to comfort the suffering animal.

Merry could see the silvery spines sticking from the hound's snout and throat. They were thicker than whiskers and quivered with each breath Tex took.

"Can't we pull them out?" she said.

"Not without hurting him more, honey. They're barbed. He needs a vet to take them out. Uncle Fern's on the phone with one."

She reached out a hand to touch the hound's shoulder.

"Better not, Merry. He's in a lot of pain. He might snap at you and not mean it."

She withdrew her hand and crouched to watch the hound's eyes, white all around with the pain.

Uncle Fern replaced the phone receiver on the wall and took a seat in a kitchen chair.

"Riverstone Vet has a van out on call up Bushmill Road.

They'll be here in an hour or more. All we can do now is keep Tex as calm as we can," he said.

"The more he moves around the deeper the quills work in," Levon said to Merry. He went back to petting the hound in slow, even strokes.

"Dumb son-bitch cornering a porcupine," Fern said. His eyes were wet with tears.

An hour and half later a four-wheel drive truck pulled up on the gravel. Instead of a bed it had a covered back with hatches along each side. On the doors were the words Riverstone Veterinary above the silhouette of a prancing horse. Uncle Fern went out to greet the vet. Merry watched through the screen door as the vet rooted around in one of the hatches along the bed and came out with a metal tool box. They walked together into the pool of light on the porch. Merry was surprised to see the vet was a woman. She was dressed in jeans and a work shirt, both stained with fresh blood. Her sandy hair was pulled back in a ponytail. The lady vet looked tired, eyes red and no makeup. For all that she was pretty to Merry's eyes. And despite the early hour and her weariness, the woman was smiling and talking easy to Uncle Fern.

"So, here's my patient, huh?" the lady vet said as she set the tool box on the kitchen table.

Merry watched as the vet crouched on the linoleum by the hound's face next to her father.

"You did good keeping him still," she said.

Levon raised his head to respond.

"Holy shit. Levon?" she said before he could speak.

"Jessie," Levon said.

"I didn't know you were back in Colby."

"Thought Dale might have told you."

"Haven't talked to Dale in years."

Levon said nothing. He guided the flat of his hand down the dog's hide in even strokes.

"I'd better see to getting these barbs out of poor Tex," Jessie said. She bent low over the whimpering dog's head with a pair of snips in her hand.

"Honey, you get on back to bed," Levon said to Merry.

Merry backed from the kitchen but did not return upstairs. She stood in the hallway, leaning against the wall to listen to the metallic snip as each barb was pinked off. Tex let out a low mewling sound as each quill was drawn out. Jessie's voice cooed to him. "There, there, boy. There's a good boy."

After a while Merry could hear the scrabble of claws on the tiles meaning Tex was back on his feet. She peeked around the corner into the kitchen. The hound galumphed over to her, tail wagging, sniffing and snorting.

"I have some antibiotics in the truck just in case. Give Tex one in the morning and one in the evening for six days." Jessie was at the sink washing her hands. She was speaking to Uncle Fern. "You may see some bleeding but that should stop in the next few hours."

Merry saw her father and he saw her.

"Thought you were in bed," he said.

"I couldn't sleep till I knew Tex was okay," Merry said.

"He's just fine, sweetheart. They stung a bit coming out but not as much as they must have been going in. He was scared is all," Jessie said. She dried her hands on a dish towel and set it by the sink.

"My name's Merry," Merry said.

"Merry Cade?" Jessie said.

"Yeah. This is my daddy."

"She's just beautiful, Levon," Jessie said. She turned back to

Merry with a smile. "I'm Jessica Hamer. I was a friend of your daddy's way back when we were both kids."

"Uh huh," Merry said. "You're a doctor now?"

"Yep. A vet. Mostly large animals like horses and cattle. But I can treat dogs and cats if they need it. But no chickens. Have to draw the line somewhere." She spoke the last with mock gravity then shared a beaming smile with Merry who giggled.

"You have a lot of blood on you," Merry said.

"I was delivering a foal on a farm near here. A beautiful dappled filly. It was already nursing by the time I got the call from the service. You like horses?"

Merry nodded with enthusiasm.

"Of course you do. What little girl doesn't? You have your daddy bring you by my place sometime soon. I have a pony that would love to have you ride her. If it's okay with you, Levon?" She turned to where Levon stood mute.

"We could. Sure," he said. "But let's not hold Jessie up any more. I'm sure she'd like to get home."

"Or stay for breakfast," Uncle Fern said. He nodded toward the windows where sunlight was slanting in through the glass.

Merry yipped. Levon gave Fern a withering glance.

"I like the beard on you, Levon," Jessie said.

"Been lazy since I got here, I guess," he said. Levon's hand went to his jaw to a two week's growth.

Over eggs, sausage, pancakes, ice cold milk and piping coffee, Merry peppered Jessie with questions while her father suffered in silence. Except for a grunt now and then to give credence to one of Jessie's stories.

Gunny Leffertz said:
"A wolf always knows when other wolves are around."

10

"Can I go horse riding at Jessie's? Can we call her? Maybe go this week?" Merry said.

"Sure, honey. Do you have the list Uncle Fern gave you?" Levon said.

"In my head," she said. Merry tapped a finger on her temple.

"It's your turn then," he said. He nodded toward the donut counter where Fay herself waited with a fold of wax paper in hand. Merry skipped forward to lean on the counter glass, raised up on her tiptoes.

"Um ... two cream-filled ... two raspberry ..."

Levon took a booth.

The place smelled of coffee brewing, fry grease and yeast. It was a smell infused into every porous surface. It smelled the same when he used to come here before or after school. When he *went* to school. Fay's mother, also Fay, ran the place then. The older Fay passed a few years back, Fern told him. The younger Fay was a shadow of her mother. Old Fay was fat as a house. Used to sit on a high stool behind the counter and sling donuts made by her husband Clyde from before dawn to late afternoon. Always smiling. Always with a greeting for everyone and the patience of a saint with customers who picked out a selection of donuts like they were making a life altering choice.

Young Fay was thin as a marathon runner and moved like a cat to pluck donuts from the tray and place them in boxes. A brush of frizzy hair held in place by a clip bobbed atop her head. Her sneakered feet squeaked on the floor boards.

Levon found a whole new generation in the little flyspeck town. The garage, the barber's, the donut shop and general store were either run by new owners or the children of the old ones. Fewer people to remember Levon Cade. Still, he pulled his Kubota ball cap low atop his dark aviators.

Only a few customers in the middle of the morning on a weekday. A couple of old guys telling war stories at the six-stool counter. Dressed in farm clothes though they probably hadn't worked the ground in decades. Both nursing coffees. They joked with the girl behind the counter. Just playful stuff. They were both old enough to be her great-grandfather. Her laughter was honest. The old guys were longtime regulars.

Two booths away a kid sat scrolling on a laptop. Hair worn long down to the collar of a Wrangler jacket with the sleeves cut away. This was the closest to Starbucks Colby had to offer.

Out the window Levon could see the wide main street with mostly pickups pulled into the angled parking spaces on either side. Three guys were hanging around an SUV on the other side of the road, smoking and sucking down beers.

They stood out. Their ride stood out. Two wore baggy jeans and outsized t-shirts. The third wore a western-style yoke shirt, skinny jeans and a straw cowboy hat. Levon didn't know much about sneakers but theirs looked expensive. Light glinted off gold chains and bracelets. Nothing about them fit in Colby.

It wasn't that they were Latinos. The county had lots of migrants working in season on the commercial farms. The migrants dressed like farm workers, dressed like most everyone else in this part of the state. Not the guys hanging around the pimped out SUV. Everything about them said gang.

The ride was a copper colored H3. It gleamed liquid in the sun with fat tires and chrome wheels with spinners. Dual chrome exhaust. A Mexican flag decal filled the rear window. The three men were young. Their body language was relaxed. One of the men bent double to laugh at a remark from another. The white fabric of a t-shirt stretched to describe an automatic in the waistband of his jeans.

"You wanted coffee, daddy?" Merry said from the counter.

"Yes, honey. A large black."

She brought the box of donuts to the table. He gave her a ten. She returned with his coffee, a small milk and change. Merry slid into the booth across from her father.

"You could have coffee at the house," she said.

"Not your uncle's coffee."

"The lady gave me a baker's dozen," Merry said and unfolded a napkin to set a donut on it.

"Because you were polite, honey."

Merry returned to the subject of horses. Levon gave her half his attention while he watched the three young men across the street. They separated after a bit. Two climbed into the Hummer. The cowboy continued on down the street to where a pickup was parked. A jacked-up Silverado with crew cab, roof lights and chrome bull bar. Jet black with a poker hand painted on the doors. All aces of spades. An ATV with knobby tires was strapped down in the bed. Both vehicles reversed onto the road. The engine sound made the glass panes of the store windows hum. They turned on the street and took off for the county road.

"So can we?" Merry was saying.

"Can we what?" Levon said. He turned his eyes from the cloud of exhaust dissolving on the street.

"Call Jessie."

"You call her and set up a day. Me or Uncle Fern can drive you over."

"I thought maybe you'd like to see her again. You and her being friends and all."

"Maybe a long time back," Levon said. He sipped his coffee. It had cooled.

"So what? You're still friends. She still likes you, right? You still like her, right?" Merry said. Her lips were white with powdered sugar. She was studying his face.

He cut his eyes back to the empty street.

"Like I said. It was a long time back. I have no idea how Jessie feels about me now. We were kids then."

"Friends are friends forever."

"It'd be nice if it was like that."

"If you don't want to take me over there..." she said. She stirred her milk with a straw.

"Of course I want you to, honey. You call and get permission and I'll take you over," he said. He reached across the table to touch her hand.

"Great," Merry said. She looked up at him, beaming.

11

"Now that the Bureau is done tripping over their own dicks we can get to work on this guy Cray," section chief Brett Sylvester said to the room at large.

"Cade," Nancy Valdez corrected.

Nancy sat at the opposite end of the conference table along with three other agents. Two of them she already knew from the DC Treasury office. Chad Bengstrom, a forensic accountant and stone wonk who could make numbers tell a story.

And Tony Marcoon, an old war horse who'd transferred over from ATF after taking a bullet in the knee during a raid. He was a former Philadelphia homicide cop and in on this case since the Blanco family had been found murdered in Costa Rica.

The third was a petite black girl in a severely cut business suit. She was on the young side and trying to project a no-bullshit, all-business attitude. This effect was undercut by large eyes and even larger horn-rimmed glasses that gave her a look of a cartoon mouse.

Brett said, "I picked this team because you're all soldiers. Your rep has been built on solid, dogged work done over long days and weeks. You do the thankless job of finding the evidence needed so the knuckleheads can go kick the doors down with their asses fully covered."

Someone cleared their throat.

"No offense meant to the knuckleheads, Tony," Brett said.

"None taken, sir," Tony Marcoon said. His voice sounded like shifting wet gravel.

"Joining you, in the spirit of inter-departmental cooperation," Brett began. There were dry chuckles. "Laura Strand is coming to this team from Internal Revenue. They have a stake in finding this guy, too. Agent Strand is on loan to us from the taxman. She worked on the team that brought down the Hester Foundation. She comes with her agency's highest recommendation."

The three Treasury agents looked at the newcomer with fresh eyes.

"The Hesters? One Gordian knot of fucked-up accounting. Props to you," Chad said.

"It was a lot of hours," Laura Strand said. A flat response, eyes level on Chad until he turned away to pretend interest in the wood grain of the tabletop. There was a silence broken only by the air conditioner hum from the ceiling of the windowless room.

Maybe she is tougher than she looks, Nancy thought.

Brett took back command of the meeting.

"You all have background on this case. Run it the way you see fit. Though I might suggest digging a little more into Cade's history. The book on this guy is suspiciously thin. I want weekly reports every Thursday by end of day. None of this sending in stuff late on Fridays bullshit." Brett's eyes cut to Chad who wore a 'who me?' expression.

"And we'll meet back here in two weeks so you can lay out your progress. We'll continue on this schedule until we've either nailed the bastard or the deputy director feels our assets would be better utilized elsewhere," Brett said. He snapped his laptop shut and pushed away from the table.

The quad would serve as the new team's HQ. It sat at the rear of the same floor as the conference room. Four desks in cubicles around a common table. There were still cartons stacked high. Equipment and paper files against the walls. Only two work stations were up and ready. Loops of cables snaked over the floor.

Chad promised their network would be booted up and running by the end of the day.

Their quad was separated from a maze of cubicles stretching across the vast floor by a wide carpeted corridor. The place had an open floor plan with hundreds of workers busy at their monitors. Still, there was a hushed tone to the place. The other agents and staff created a waxing and waning sound like a distant surf.

"I've been the longest on the forensic end of this so I'll take lead," Nancy said.

She took a seat at the head of the table. Chad flipped open his laptop and was immediately tapping away. Nancy had worked with him before and knew he was taking in everything she said even if he appeared to be lost to cyberland. Tony sat regarding her with heavy eyelids. Laura Strand had a notepad open and pen poised to take notes.

"We'll attack this from several different angles," Nancy said. "First up is to build a history on Levon Cade. Like Brett said, his file is thin. We need to know more about him. Something might tell us where he is now."

Chad tapped. Tony nodded. Laura Strand jotted.

"We're going to keep up our sweep for any currency popping up connected to the Blanco stash. We're had a few hits but not enough to create a pattern."

"The bills that have been reported point south," Chad said.

"We just got a call on a hundred note in Montreal. I need you to enter that in our system," Nancy said.

Chad blew air through his lips.

"Next we're going to do as deep a forensic analysis of the late Corey Blanco as we can. Really grind it out to create a full picture of his holdings. There might be something there we can use. An angle. A chink in the armor. That way we'll have a full inventory of funds we can possibly seize. There's a lot of stolen loot to be found and a shitload of tax dollars to be recovered."

"How's that help us find Cade?" Tony said.

"It's more to justify our continued existence," Nancy said. "If we can establish a dollar amount on what Blanco was holding then we can make the deputy director understand why we need to keep digging."

"What's to say this guy Cade can lead us to the Blanco stash?" Laura Strand said.

"We know there's a key, some form of a code or a device, that Blanco used as an index to his offshore accounts," Nancy said. "Our working theory is Cade has the key."

"I understand the key exists," Laura Strand said. "The home invasion crew broke into the Blanco home in Costa Rica but left millions in cash and valuables behind. They didn't find what they were looking for because Corey Blanco died of a massive heart attack while they were torturing his family. The crew then broke into another Blanco home in Fiji, again leaving millions in swag behind."

"Then they show up in—" Laura Strand flipped pages in her notebook, "—Bellevue Lake, Maine. Another Blanco home. Another home invasion. They run into a handyman who kills the entire crew before vanishing with a few million in cash, his eleven-year-old daughter and, theoretically, this key to billions in stolen funds."

"That's the reason why we're here. And it's more than theoretical," Nancy said. "We have confirmation from Kiera Anne Blanco-Reeves, a Blanco ex-wife. She's made a statement that Cade took more than cash from the house. She also has her own experience of her husband's practices to back up the idea of a load of hidden assets."

"What about this crew?" Tony said. "Do we have more on them?"

"There's a fat file from the FBI on all of them. Mostly Belgian nationals. All professional career thieves. High-end scores only," Nancy said.

"They went global in their search for the Blanco stash. That takes start-up money. There's no way they did it on their own dime. Someone financed them," Tony said.

"And gave them intel. Corey Blanco was burrowed deep," Nancy said.

"Maybe we're not the only ones looking for Cade?" Laura Strand said.

"I think we can safely assume that," Nancy said.

"Then we better make sure we find this fucker first," Laura said. She smiled. A feral, lupine leer. The cartoon mouse was gone.

Gunny Leffertz said:
"A man can only hide his true game so long."

12

"You're just in time," Levon said.

He stepped from the shade of the carport to meet Dale pulling onto the gravel. Dale stepped out of the cab and waded through the trio of sniffing hounds. The day was a hot one, summer coming on early.

"You gonna get that old thing running again?" Dale said. He waved a hand at the Mustang, now uncovered, in the carport. The car was dappled in patches of pink and gray primer. The original metallic green finish was faded. The windshield had a crack down the center. The hood was off revealing an engine crusted with rust.

Uncle Fern stepped out into the sunlight. Feller trotted alongside him.

"Got the wheels back on. I could use your help pushing her into the garage," Levon said.

"Sure," Dale said. He shrugged out of his uniform shirt and tossed it to the hood of the car. He wore a white tank top underneath. No body armor. His arms were thick with muscle gone to flab. They were sleeved with tattoos from wrists to shoulder. The largest was an angry cartoon ram charging above a scroll reading 'Mountain Pride.' A big numeral one was on one forearm in red ink with 'Army Strong' emblazoned beneath it.

The two men pushed the car clear of the carport and angled it toward the open barn doors. With Uncle Fern walking alongside, reaching in to turn the wheel, they pushed the Mustang into the barn against a two-by-four stop nailed to the floor boards. A chain hoist was rigged up from a roof beam ready to haul the engine clear. A steel engine stand stood off to one side. A brand new Makita compressor and a shiny chest of new air-powered tools were set nearby.

Dale leaned on the trunk, sucking in breath. His tank top was sopping. His hair was dark with sweat. Levon offered him a longneck from a cooler packed with ice.

"You want one or are you on duty?" he said.

"In this heat? I'll sweat it off," Dale said and popped the top to take a long swallow.

"Thanks for helping. Would have been a bitch pushing this alone," Levon said.

"Alone? What the hell am I?" Fern said. He gestured with a beer of his own.

"You, old man? Like Levon wants to spend the summer listening to you bitch about your thrown back," Dale said. He tipped the bottle and drained it in one go.

"What brings you out here?" Levon said.

"Lester Murdock saw some fat hogs up along the ridge near the colored cemetery. Sows and a big old male. Thought maybe you'd like to come see if we can find them."

"Swine season's not till November. Or don't deputies follow the same rules as the rest of us?"

"Just a stalk, Goose. Just a look-see."

"We'll be back by six? Merry's coming back then."

"Where's she at?" Dale said.

"Horseback riding. She's spending the day at the stables," Levon said.

"Jessie's place," Uncle Fern said.

Levon cut him a look. Fern only laughed.

"Jessie Gillis? You picking up where you left off?" Dale said. His face creased with amusement.

"She's Jessie Hamer now. Offered to teach Merry to ride, is all." Levon shrugged.

"Seems I remember the two of you doing some ridin' on your own back in the day," Dale said. His grin broadened to show his back teeth.

Uncle Fern sprayed beer before breaking into a choking cackle. His face turned red.

"All right. I'll go stalk some swine if it'll shut you up," Levon said. He scooped the uniform shirt off the hood and tossed it to Dale.

"I'm a little late getting started today. I'll saddle the horses then we'll go for a ride," Jessie said.

"I want to help," Merry said, trotting after Jessie across the paddock.

"You sure?"

"I want to learn how to put a saddle on. And how to brush them and all."

"It's a lot of work," Jessie said. She stepped into the tidy six-stall stable. A heavy scent of animal presence hung in the air; a wet smell with a tang of cloying sweetness.

"I don't care. I love being around horses," Merry said. She stooped to pat the head of a springer spaniel with a spastic tail.

A teenaged girl stepped from a stall with a forkful of horse droppings. She flipped the fork to dump them into a wheelbarrow already piled high with dung and wet sawdust. She was a skinnier junior version of Jessie in overalls, wellies and Starbucks t-shirt.

"This is Merry, Sandy. This is Sandy. My little girl. We're taking out Brewster and Montana today," Jessie said.

"Hey. I'd shake your hand but it's covered in shit," Sandy said. Her voice was dry, with a lazy drawl deeper than her mother's.

Merry giggled. The ghost of a smile on Sandy's face evaporated as fast as it appeared.

"Merry is into it. She wants to help me saddle and groom and the whole mess," Jessie said. She reached over a stall door with a bridle. The head of a cinnamon colored quarter horse loomed over the door. Jessie patted the horse's neck and made clucking noises as she slid the bridle in place.

"You got a case of horse fever, huh?" Sandy said.

"Don't you? You get to live around them every day, right?" Merry said.

"They're big, stupid animals that need hay shoveled in one end and shit shoveled on the other."

"So why do you do it?"

"For money. My mom let me have four stalls. I rent them out to boarders. They pay extra for feeding and mucking."

"You don't own your own horse?" Merry said.

"Mom lets me ride Brewster if I want. Montana used to be my pony before I outgrew him," Sandy said. She picked up the poles of the barrow and rolled it to the next stall.

Jessie had the quarter horse cross-tied in the aisle between the stalls. She called Merry over to show her how the saddle pad and saddle were put on and how to make sure it was cinched tight. They left Brewster standing, huffing softly, and brought out Montana, a buckskin pony with a dark mane and tail. Jessie put the bridle on then took it off and allowed Merry to put it on. Slipping the bit between the teeth and over the tongue was the hardest part. The sleepy looking pony seemed to be helping.

"Montana's an old hack pony. She takes the bit easier than most. Makes her the best one to practice on," Jessie said.

Merry placed the pad on the pony's back with Jessie's aid. She insisted on putting the saddle on herself. Looping the stirrup up on the pommel and going up on tiptoes to set it just right. They were riding western. The saddle was worn, broken in, but gleamed with polish.

"Don't be afraid of getting it too tight. You're not going to hurt her as long as the cinch is in the right place," Jessie said.

Merry pulled the strap through the rings and secured it with a little help. Jessie tested the tautness with a tug.

"Not bad for the first time. You might just be a natural," Jessie said, stepping back.

They led the mounts out into the sunlight. Merry wore a smile that almost hurt, her fist tight on the reins.

"We're just going on a little trail ride, okay? There's a community trail runs around the subdivision a few miles," Jessie said.

Merry nodded, eager.

"If you like this and want to ride more you need to tell Levon to buy you some riding boots." Jessie nodded at Merry's Doc Martin's.

"I know I'm going to love it," Merry said.

"Well, then, let's ride."

Jessie steadied the pony while Merry lifted up in the stirrup and threw a leg over with ease.

"Like I said. A natural," Jessie said.

Gunny Leffertz said:
"War's different for every man. Some come out worse. Some better. Some the same. It's a fire that burns or tempers. All depends on the man."

13

Dale braked the county truck to a stop on a switchback road that climbed a thirty degree grade to just shy of the ridge line. It was a rutted path nearly invisible under the cover of a carpet of ferns. The way ahead was blocked by a big old poplar fallen across the path.

"This is as far as we go on wheels, Goose. We hike the rest." Dale killed the engine and climbed out. He wore his uniform shirt unbuttoned.

Levon got out the other side and stood scanning the deep woods around them. Dale shoved the bench seat forward to reveal a gun rack bolted to the rear wall of the cab. He pulled a shotgun from the loops. A semi-auto model with an extended tube magazine and pistol grip.

"A Beretta. Those things cost money," Levon said.

"You get what you pay for. You want to carry? Help yourself," Dale said. He gestured to a Remington pump and a nicked up old Winchester lever action resting in the other loops on the rack.

"That's okay. I'll go unarmed," Levon lied.

"Up to you," Dale said. He pushed the seat back in place and shut the cab door. He clicked the remote, locking the truck with a double tweet.

Dale led the way forward up the hill.

"It's not far. Just past the headstones in a high draw," he said.

Levon followed. The woods were quiet but for the rising and

falling chirrup of cicadas in the trees. A cloud of white moths glided over the tops of the ferns. Above them the canopy was filling in with green shoots of new leaves as the warm weather returned.

As they passed the fallen poplar Levon saw it had not surrendered to rot. Fresh white wood where a straight cut from a chain saw had dropped it across the trail.

Dale was panting within moments, fighting to climb the increasing angle of the incline.

"You're not Army strong anymore," Levon said. Levon was walking and breathing easy.

"You got the good genes, I guess," Dale said. He looked back, smiling. His face was shiny with sweat.

"You got the same genes, Dale."

"Different mama, Goose."

"How's the department feel about you letting yourself turn to goo?"

"It's not like the army. We ain't paramilitary up here. Just pulling over drunk drivers and shit. Easy duty."

"No excuse to go all to hell. You used to be all-county. Used to leave me in the dust running cross-country."

Dale stopped and squatted to put his back to a tree. He pulled a pack of Pall Malls from his shirt and started one up. He sucked in a lungful and let it out slow. Levon took a knee near him.

"I could blame Iraq, I guess. That be the pussy thing to do. Got on pain pills after I got busted up. They took their hold. I was a while cleaning up. Cassie took off on me then. Can't blame her."

Levon said nothing.

"Bet you think I broke my hip falling over my own big feet. I got busted up when the truck I was riding in got flipped by an IED. Big ass truck loaded with me and my buddies went ass over like a toy, man. Compound fracture to my femur. I got a plastic hip and a shitload of pins and plates now." Dale slapped his left leg.

Levon sat, his back to the ridge line.

"Most of my buddies got burned alive. I don't know if I crawled clear or was pulled clear. Got some burns on my legs. Nothing like some of those boys. I was three months in traction after God alone knows how many surgeries. Then they packed me home with painkillers and a medical discharge."

"Looks like you recovered all right," Levon said.

"Guess so. Cassie left. I kicked the pills with some help from the NA. Church of Christ holds meetings down in Haley three nights a week. The county took me on, me being a vet an' all."

"It's a long way back."

"And what about you? You ever find your way back? Back here hiding in the woods from damn near every government agency that's got a name? Who'd you piss off?"

"Everybody, I guess," Levon said.

"Least you have your little girl."

"She's something to go on for."

"Yeah." Dale took the last drag from the cigarette. He smeared the butt cold on his boot heel before picking up the shotgun and rising to his feet.

They climbed until the incline eased, coming to a more level bit of ground. Through the boles of young beeches they could see the humps of grave markers above the undergrowth. Sections of a rusted wrought iron fence, knee high, still stood in places. An old cemetery from way back in the days of segregation. No one was sure how long ago. The families moved to the cities or moved north many years past. The names and stories of the men and women buried here forgotten a long time ago.

The wind rising up the other side of the ridge stirred the tops of the trees. Something rode up with the wind. A sharp chemical scent.

"Smells like paint thinner and piss. Someone have a still down there?" Levon said. He paused in the forest gloom, sniffing.

"Not a still. No one's had a thumper up here in a long while," Dale said. Voice low. Listening. He stopped, head turning on a swivel.

"There's a fire road down there. The one off Turner Mill," Levon said.

"Coming back to you, huh?"

"Yeah. What's coming back to me is that the holler is dry down there. Has been since the Lipscomb Dam was finished."

Dale was turned away, not meeting Levon's eyes.

"This ain't hog country," Levon said.

Dale said nothing. He kept looking down the slope below them into the swaying limbs. A wispy haze of vapor rose through the sprouting leaves. It carried with it the acid stink of toxins.

"What's this about, Dale?" Levon stepped closer.

"Those are meth labs down there. Whole shitpot of them. Used to be run by the Pettit cousins. Remember them? You used to run with Ty Pettit. They're all gone now. Now it's a crew of Mexicans. And they don't play."

"So what's this mean to me?"

"Thought you'd want to know who your neighbors are. Those labs are just a spit away from Uncle Fern's place as the crow flies."

"You expect me to do something about it?"

"You're one who's supposed to be the hard man, brother. Thought you might like to give me a hand," Dale said. He faced Levon, face pinched in a sour expression.

"Isn't this a police matter, Dale?"

"I ain't police any more, Goose. County let me go a few months back."

Dale turned back to look downhill once more. Levon stared at his half-brother, taking in the pain on the man's face.

14

"Were you like my daddy's girlfriend?" Merry said.

"For a while. When we were kids," Jessie said.

They were riding easy, the horses walking, on a tamped dirt trail through the trees.

"Before he met my mom?"

"Long time before."

"But you still like him."

"Sure I do. Though he's different now."

"How's he different?"

"Quieter, I guess. He used to be a real clown. I mean funny. Always making me laugh."

"Funny?" Merry said. There was deep wonder in her voice.

"You've known him all your life. But I've known him most of mine," Jessie said. "He was very different then."

"He changed some after my mom died, too. But he never smiled much even before," Merry said. Her head bobbed along as she rode.

The trail turned from the trees to follow the grading along train tracks. The rails were orange with rust. Weeds grew up between the ties. The crunch of gravel echoed off a high wall of chipped rock on the other side of the tracks.

"What about Sandy's daddy? Is he a clown, too?" Merry said.

"He was sometimes. He passed a while back. When Sandy was a little girl," Jessie said.

"I'm sorry. I didn't know."

"It's okay. He was in the Army. A Ranger. We lost him in Afghanistan."

They rode quiet a while through bars of sunlight coming down between the trees.

"Where we lived before? In Huntsville?" Merry said. "None of the kids' daddies were in the military. But since we came to Uncle Fern's it seems all the daddies were."

"That's what it's like up here," Jessie said. "So many of the men go to war. Always been the way. I read once the only group who join up more than mountain folks is American Indians."

"I wonder why that is."

"Hard to think of why. Two people as hard used as us and the Indians. I guess it's a love of the country, the idea of a free country. A sense of duty."

"My mom used to say my daddy just liked to fight."

Jessie laughed. It startled her mount who huffed in reply.

"There's that too. Stupid men," she said.

They made their way back down the slope, moving sideways on the steeper runs. Boots braced so as not to slide.

"You're just playing at being a deputy now?" Levon said.

"Bought the truck at auction. I was supposed to sand off the insignia. Didn't get around to it," Dale said.

"And the uniform?"

"Only wear the shirt sometimes. Not like I'm going armed."

The slope eased to a ten degree run. They found the jeep trail and walked toward where they left Dale's truck.

"Quit or fired?" Levon said. He tried to stay even with Dale to read his face. Dale stayed just ahead, Levon on his blindside.

"They let me quit. They didn't want any trouble," Dale said.

"What did you do?"

"Looked out for some people. People you and me known all our lives."

"Turning a blind eye's not the job, Dale."

"You don't know what it's like, Goose."

"So tell me."

Dale stopped and turned back to Levon. His eyes were red. His mouth a twisted wound.

"Everything's changed. Used to be the county left us alone," Dale said. He was fighting to keep his voice even. "Let the hills be the hills, you know? 'Cause the deputies and alla them used to be us, you know. Our neighbors. They understood."

"I remember. It was the state police gave our daddy and Uncle Fern a hard time. They did what they wanted in county. Especially Daddy," Levon said.

"All over with now, Goose. By the by. The sheriff's over from Tolliver County. Held chicken dinners and hung signs every damned where. The deputies are all like college boys up from Birmingham and Huntsville. They're not us. They don't give a shit about us."

Levon said nothing.

"They sent me for training down to Bush Hills. Like boot camp for pussies. I took classes in law enforcement. They had an instructor there teaching about the 'special challenges' of working in rural areas. He talked about how hard it was to build a case up in here. Said the biggest obstacle a cop faced was 'mountain pride.' You believe it? Told us we had to break that pride to make everyone behave right."

"They're only enforcing the law."

"Look at who's talking!" Dale said. "Mister FBI most wanted!"

"Not the same thing."

"No? Hell, boy, they got you on terror lists with fuckers like the ones blew me up in Iraq."

"Way I see it, the sheriff used to cover for our daddy. Looked the other way when he beat my mom and yours. A little law, a little time in the county pen would have done him good. Would have done us good, for sure."

Dale's eyes narrowed to slits. His mouth turned to a lipless line. His knuckles turned white on the shotgun.

"Fuck you," Dale said. He turned to walk down the hill. Levon let him have some distance, waiting to follow.

He came up on Dale standing at the barrier of the downed poplar. Levon trotted up to join him.

The county truck sat on its rims, tires slashed flat. In the ferns along the road a pair of ATVs squatted, the riders nowhere to be seen.

Gunny Leffertz said:
"Know your enemy. Know yourself. Know the ground. But most of all, know the goddamned ground."

15

"Hold up and listen." Levon's voice was low. He put a hand on Dale's arm.

They ducked low behind the felled tree bole.

"You got a round chambered?" Levon said.

Dale worked the action lever back a bit to reveal a fat round in place. Levon nodded.

Footfalls in the underbrush to their left. The brittle squawk of a radio voice to their right.

"We wait till they're back together," Levon said. His voice wasn't above a hiss.

A voice responded to the radio call. The same voice called out to another.

"El nos dice que vaya a la colina."

"Mierde." A second man to the left.

Levon leaned on the bole listening to the footfalls converge on the trail. He held a hand up to Dale. Dale's eyes were wide, his teeth clenched in a snarl. His face ran with fresh sweat.

The engines of the ATVs whined to life. The tires spun, spitting gravel. The noise closed on Levon and Dale. The riders were approaching to pass around the fallen tree in the woods to either side.

Levon slapped Dale's shoulder and stood to move to his right. As he moved he cleared the 1911 from its place at the small of his back. It slid easy from the oiled pancake holster in his waistband. An ATV was banking around the tree stump. The rider looked like the cowboy he saw in Colby the week before. The man stared in stunned surprise at the bearded white man rising up before him.

The boom of the shotgun joined the triple tap of the .45. The hollow points struck the cowboy square in the chest, then neck, then face. Levon allowed the big auto to climb as he fired. The rider went backward off the saddle. A sneaker flipped high in the air. The ATV trundled on to a stop in the ferns.

Levon was turning before his target struck the ground. Dale was firing a second and third charge toward the second ATV. The driver's head split like a melon. He slid from the vehicle to tumble back down the slope. A second man, riding behind, pitched himself to the ground. His white t-shirt was stained crimson with blood.

The second ATV rolled to a halt against the fallen tree. The engine died. Levon leaped over the bole to run for the third man crawling through the ferns on his belly.

Two rounds in the back brought the man to a halt. A third opened his skull in a spray. Dale finished the second driver with a round of buck to the head.

Levon rushed up to the bitch rider. Inches from the dead man's fingers lay a tricked-out AR-15. It went flying when the pair were first struck by the loads of buck from Dale's Beretta.

Dale stood breathing heavy over his target. Levon swung his arm in a stirring motion for his half-brother to keep an eye out.

The bitch rider wore a Glock in a tooled holster against his spine. Levon stripped off the action, released the mag and threw the three parts deep into the woods before picking up the custom rifle. His first observation was wrong. The rifle was an M4, capable of full auto fire. It had all the toys mounted on its rail system. 10x scope. Maglite. Forward grip. The barrel was chromed as were the magazine, trigger guard and front half-ring sight.

He trotted to the cowboy and took a .357 Colt from a belly holster. There was a second M4, a stripped down military issue model, strapped across the handlebars. He removed it and slung it over his shoulder with the first one. In the small cargo compartment he found three full mags. He stuck them in the back pockets of his jeans.

Levon moved to the second ATV sitting where it crashed into the fallen tree. He found a Tech-9 in the boot. He stripped it to four parts and tossed them as far as he could in four different directions. Deeper in the boot were four more M4 mags. All chromed. He trotted to join Dale and handed him the four mags and the pimped out rifle. He stooped to pat down the headless man at Dale's feet.

"You told me you weren't armed," Dale said.

"You told me there was pigs out here," Levon said.

"Shouldn't we be moving on?"

"On four flat tires?"

"Someone might have heard those shots."

"Gunfire's nothing unusual in these woods. It wouldn't carry far over the ridge anyway."

"What're we doing here, Goose?" Dale said. He slung the shotgun over his shoulder and stood cradling the rifle and magazines in his arms.

"I could ask you the same damned thing," Levon said. He turned up a Czech nine millimeter under the dead man's t-shirt. He shoved it in his waistband.

"Meaning what?" Dale said. The color was returning to his face.

"You brought me up here to stalk pigs only you knew they weren't here. You wanted me to know about those meth kitchens. Maybe you can tell me why."

"Can't you see why? We go for a walk in the woods and nearly wind up dead. We ran these woods day and night when we were kids. You can't see what's going on?"

"I see what I see."

"I told you Ty Pettit was run off. He wasn't. These son-bitches killed him. Cut his head off. His wife too. His brother packed up and left the county the next day."

"There's police to handle that."

"You think so? Well, they've done jack shit about it," Dale said. "Handed it onto the state. The case is just a folder in a file now."

Levon stood waiting for more.

"Nobody in these hills will help the law. Not even with a bunch of outsiders running around cutting throats and setting fire to houses. Ain't nobody going to do a damned thing."

"Mountain pride."

"So proud they'll choke on it."

Levon turned to the headless man at Dale's feet and pulled up his t-shirt. The first load of buck had taken him in the gut exposing pink meat and white bone. The unwounded flesh was covered in a skein of black tattoos unreadable under a coat of drying blood. He pulled up the sleeve on one arm. At the shoulder was a grinning skull with a smoking joint clamped in its teeth. An ornate letter 'Z' was at the center of the skull's forehead. In a scroll beneath it was 'Tamaulipas.' A gulf coast state in Mexico.

"That doesn't stand for Zorro," Levon said.

"Zetas cartel. Shit."

"What was your plan here, Dale?"

"To scare them off." Dale's voice was small.

"They're in the scaring *business*."

Dale looked away. Levon turned at a sound from nearby.

The click and squawk of a radio.

"Rudy? *Dónde estás, prima?*"

Gunny Leffertz said:
> *"Maybe you didn't ask for trouble but trouble asked for you. Man up, wire your shit tight and take a run at that trouble double time."*

16

Levon plucked a two-way radio from the cowboy's belt.

He held it away from him, listening to a voice calling for an answer.

He pressed the send button home.

"*Cállate! Que no es nada!*" Levon said. He barked the words in Mexican-accented Spanish.

"Okay, Rudy. *Cuando vas a volver aquí?*" the radio said after a pause.

"*No puedo escucharte*," Levon said. He clicked the radio off and hooked it to his own belt.

"Damn, brother," Dale said. "You fucking sound like a fucking wetback."

"No one should come looking for them for a while. Buys us some time." Levon stood up and checked his rifle to make sure it was charged and combat ready. He adjusted the nylon sling so the M4 hung rigged across his torso.

"Time to do what?"

"You wanted to scare them? Let's go scare them." Levon moved past the fallen poplar to trot back toward the ridge line.

"Start at the neck and pull the comb back along the flank," Jessie said.

Montana was cross-tied in the stable. Merry used a hooped

steel curry to comb the dust from his hair. The pony stamped a hoof and huffed through its nostrils.

"Not his belly. He's ticklish," Jessie said.

"Do you ever give them baths?" Merry said. She caressed the animal with a gentle hand as she combed.

"We hose them off. But only earlier in the day. The nights are still cool. Can't be putting them up wet."

"Do they like this? Like us fussing over them?"

"They *love* it. They're all divas, horses. They eat up the attention worse than dogs."

Jessie unhooked the reins and let Merry lead the pony back to his stall. She helped the little girl unhook the bridle. They closed the stall door and Montana trotted over for one last pat on the muzzle, lips slapping over champing teeth.

"So, you like riding?" Jessie said.

"I want to do it every day," Merry said. There was such a plain earnestness to the statement that Jessie let out a whoop of laughter.

"I'll bet you're hurting."

"My butt's sore, I guess."

"You'll feel it in your legs and back come morning. Riding is real exercise. They're carrying us but they're not doing all the work."

"Can you talk my daddy into buying me my own pony?" Merry said. There was a gleam in her eye.

"Hold on now. I want your father to still think of me as a friend," Jessie said. "You're the one who should ask him. And maybe wait till you have had a few lessons first. Make sure you want to do this."

An insistent buzzing came from the pocket of Jessie's barn coat slung on a stall post. She pulled her cell phone free. The number on the display looked odd to her.

It was Levon.

"Jessie, I hate to ask. Something's come up and I won't be by to pick up Merry when I said. Can you run her back to my Uncle Fern's?"

"Well, if you're going to be a few hours she could just stay here and have dinner with us."

"Can I speak to her?"

Jessie handed the phone to Merry who listened, a smile widening on her face.

"Sure, Daddy. That would be awesome. Love you too." Merry ended the call and handed the phone back to Jessie.

"He said it's okay with him if it's okay with you," Merry said.

"I promised Sandy pizza tonight. Maybe we'll all run into Haley after we've fed and watered."

"Can I help? Can I?" Merry said.

"Sandy was right. You do have it bad, Merry Cade," Jessie said.

"We coulda took those Yamahas," Dale said. He was blown and panting, his back to a tree at the peak of the ridge.

"They'd be looking for their friends then," Levon said. He was on a knee to wait for Dale to catch his breath. He replaced the sat phone in his jacket pocket.

"Going to be dark soon." Dale lipped the filter of a Pall Mall and slid it from the crumpled pack.

Levon yanked the cigarette from his mouth, crushed it, and tossed the flakes aside before making his way down the hill into the cover of the trees.

"Shit," Dale said. He trotted after his half-brother.

He caught up. Levon moved sure over a spill of gray rocks scattered down the slope. Dale watched his footing, hopping from surface to surface.

"What do we do when we get down there?" Dale said.

"We clean this up," Levon said.

"You saying what I think you're saying?"

"The guy with the comms might have called in your plate number. No more talking from here on. Maintain noise discipline."

Dale stopped to wipe his forehead dry on a shirt sleeve. He rechecked his rifle's load. He watched Levon drop off a shelf of rock into a copse of birches.

"Goddamn," he said. It was a curse and a prayer.

Gunny Leffertz said:
"Surprise is a bitch. Make sure she's on your side."

17

The sun dropped behind the hills leaving the valley in green shadow under a still blue sky.

Levon found a brush of scrub pines on a piece of level ground. He dropped to his belly to scan the buildings below through the 10x scope mounted on the M4. Dale scrambled up on knees and elbows to lie beside him, breathing hard.

Three buildings sat in a cleft at the end of a road of packed dirt leading away through the brush toward the north-south fire road. They were simple structures of stacked block. Metal rooftops. Steel casement windows. The kind of shacks migrant workers lived in during picking season. Except this compound was miles from any commercial farm.

The other difference was an untidy heap of plastic barrels and jugs lying in a growth of sumac. The chemical ingredients of a recipe for crystal meth. And the smell. It was stronger here, trapped on the floor of the holler by the surrounding slopes. The sharp sting of paint spirits and the musk of animal urine. It coated the back of the throat and created a sting in the nostrils.

Nothing moved below. There were signs the shacks weren't abandoned. A Kia sport vehicle parked between two buildings. Vapor rose from a stove pipe set in the roof of the largest building. Music played somewhere. A Mexican pop song. A *corrido* about some brave drug kingpin battling the police to protect his *hacienda*. It came from one of the two smaller structures. A bunk house maybe.

Levon nudged closer to his half-brother to place his face close to Dale's ear.

"We wait till it gets darker. Try to get a census."

Dale nodded.

"I need you to cover the SUV. No one drives out of here."

Dale swallowed hard. He nodded again.

"Rest if you need it. I'll keep watch till it's time." Levon moved back to his first position.

A sudden wave of exhaustion washed over Dale. It was like Levon's words gave him permission to surrender to the aches in his legs and arms and back. That wasn't it. Dale was a soldier too. Three deployments to Iraq, he knew it was adrenaline leeching from his body at the first moment of quiet since they opened up on those three guys. He set the rifle and shotgun aside and rested his head on his arm.

Scratchy squawks came from the walkie in Levon's hand. The volume down, Levon was keying the radio to make the guys down in the shacks think their dead amigos were still trying to send. A muted voice bleated from the radio a few times between clacks and clicks. Even at low volume Dale could hear the irritation in the tinny voice though he could not hear the words. Wouldn't understand them if he did.

He drifted off to the rhythm of radio hiss and whispered gibberish. In a dream Dale was riding in an '83 T-bird with the roof off. Rick Mueller, his best buddy in high school, was driving. It was the car they both always talked about owning. One badass ride. The road was straight and flat with desert stretched out to the horizon in all directions. Dale put his head back on the head rest, squinting through his Oakleys at the sun glinting off the hood.

"When we gonna get to Vegas, Ricky?" he said.

"We're not going to Vegas," Rick Mueller said.

He was in crisp new BDUs. Digi-desert pattern. Bucket on his head all strapped down.

Dale looked down the highway. The signs coming toward them were in Arabic.

"So where we going?" Dale said.

"You know where," Rick Mueller said. He punched the accelerator. The big eight roared higher.

"Can I get out now? Can you pull over?"

"No way. We got to go," Rick Mueller said. He was laughing when he said it.

Dale sat up in the dark. His head brushed low branches. It was full dark. A hand gripped his arm. Another clapped over his mouth. Levon's voice low, close to his ear.

"I count five. Five I could see. Nod if you understand."

Dale nodded. The hand came away from his mouth. Levon's voice continued.

"I'm moving down to the left. You move right. Get close to the car."

"Uh huh."

"Don't let anyone near the car. Okay? We clear on that?"

"Yeah."

"You have one job, Dale. Don't fuck it up."

"I won't."

"Move now," Levon said and slipped away into the scrub.

Dale rose to a crouch. His knees ached. He made a last check of the shotgun and rifle. Rounds chambered. Safeties off. The Beretta was slung over his back. The M4 in his fists. He willed himself to move to the right and clear of the pines. He made his way down toward where he recalled the SUV was parked.

Golden light glowed from the casement windows of two of the buildings. Somewhere a gas generator throbbed. Voices in Spanish came from one of the shacks. Thin voices from a speaker.

As he got closer he heard a wave of laughter from an audience. One of the bunkhouses pulsed with the blue glow of a television inside.

He dropped to the cover of a thick tree bole surrounded by a thick skirt of ivy at its base. He had a clear line of fire toward the Kia sitting fifty feet from the nearest shack. Dale dropped to one knee and sighted over the rifle held to his shoulder. His ears reached out for fresh sounds. His eyes searched for any movement in blackness between the collection of buildings.

Dale's clothes were damp with sweat. His mouth was arid dry. He knew the feeling. He'd been here before more times than he could count. He shook off the chill. He worked his mouth to make a few drops of spit. It was hours since his last cigarette. It surprised him. He'd forgotten all about the pack of Pall Malls crinkling in his shirt pocket.

The canned laughter rose in volume in response to a shrill voice in Spanish from the television. "*Esa fue mi hermana!*"

A cracking sound echoed from the shacks. It was followed by a rapid series of pops and cracks. Levon was working his M4 somewhere inside the collection of buildings. Dale sighted his rifle. No signs of movement. More sounds reached him. The pop-pop-pop of Levon's mike-four was answered by the throaty roar of a larger bore weapon. Followed by the chugging of what Dale knew to be a Kalashnikov being fired on full auto. A trio of red tracers arced up over the rooftops to vanish in the trees. The AK went silent.

Voices, real voices, rose now. Men shouted urgent commands. Curses.

Shadows fluttered against the wall of a shack. The voices were clearer now, reaching Dale over the open ground. A man ran into view, sped along by a fresh explosion of fire from Levon's rifle. The man was naked but for a pair of bikini underwear slung under a belly that wobbled as he ran. The sight might have been comical except for the black shape of a weapon in his hand.

Dale sighted before the man, laying the tang midway between the running figure and the Kia. In the splinter of time before he pressed the trigger home he saw the man had something clenched in his teeth. It jangled with a metallic sound. A key chain.

A three round burst fired a tick to the lead of the running man. The guy ran headlong into the rounds, going down screaming with shots to his legs. Still screaming, the man pulled himself along the ground by his hands toward the Kia. Dale stood for a better angle and sent another three round burst into the fallen man's center mass. The man lay still.

A boom followed by flying wood chips and bark raining on Dale's head and shoulders. A man stood in the partial cover of a corner of the nearest shack. He was pumping a fresh round into a shotgun. Dale returned fire as he dropped. The shots went wild. The shotgun man, emboldened, stepped from cover. He had the shotgun raised to his shoulder, barrel trained lower now. He racked and fired three charges of buck in as many seconds.

Shot whistled past Dale, snapping the tops from the milkweeds he lay in for cover. He lay on his side throwing fire toward the shotgun man who was haring for the Kia. The guy was a cool one, popping rounds into the pump gun as he moved. He was almost to the door of the vehicle. Dale's rounds chased him in a sweeping arc but none connected.

The shotgun man paused in mid-flight. He looked like someone who was planning a road trip and had the thought he'd forgotten something. His legs folded under him and he dropped to the weeds.

"Coming to you!" Levon's voice clear in the sudden silence.

Levon moved from the cover of the shacks at a fast walk. The M4 shouldered. He fired two controlled bursts at the place where the shotgun man had dropped. He kept moving forward, pumping two rounds into the near-naked guy at point blank range.

"Clear." Levon stood scanning the darkness. The rifle was lowered to his chest. From one of the shacks came mariachi music. Blaring horns and a man singing in a trilling tenor.

Dale stood on shaking legs to walk toward Levon.

"You okay?" Levon said.

"I think so," Dale said. He looked down at himself. No bleeds. He didn't hurt anywhere but he knew that meant nothing.

"There were seven. These two are the last."

"This one has the car keys." Dale tilted his chin at the white figure lying face down in the weeds. Blood gleamed black on the flabby flesh. Dale stood panting. He could feel his heartbeat driving hard in his arms and his neck.

"You all right, Dale?" Levon stooped to pick up the key chain gleaming silver in the moonlight.

"Sure. Fucking A. I feel great." And he did. The aftermath of an adrenaline rush combined with the familiar thrill of having gone into a shit storm and come out the other end alive. He laughed and put his hand over his mouth to muffle it.

"You know what?" he said. "I've never been more hungry in my life."

"Good. Means you're alive." Levon turned to head back to the shacks.

"Where we going?" Dale said. He trotted to Levon's side.

"We're not done here."

Gunny Leffertz said:
> *"Killing men is work. Don't ever let anyone tell you different."*

18

The largest building was the lab. Another was a kind of barracks with steel frame bunkbeds enough for eight men. The smallest was storage, as well as what looked like a common room. This was where the television was along with a card table and chairs and an aging, sprung seat sofa. A mini-fridge and a microwave were in the corner of a makeshift kitchen area. There were five-gallon plastic drums stacked against a wall.

Two men lay dead on the floor by collapsed chairs. It looked like they were snacking on milk and cookies and watching television when Levon surprised them. They were young guys lying in a mix of spattered milk and their own blood. A shotgun leaned against the wall by the door. Out of reach when the shit came down. Might as well have been on the moon.

Levon stepped over them to snap the TV off. The silence left behind was filled by the returning cadence of night noises from the woods. Cicadas and toads.

Dale helped himself to an unopened bag of cream sandwich cookies he found in a cabinet. He washed them down with a can of Coors he found in a cooler. Nothing ever tasted so good.

Levon popped the top of one of the plastic drums. It was filled with sealed plastic baggies of equal weight containing what looked like powdery white rocks. Crystal meth. This was the product of the on-site lab. Millions of dollars' worth in a dozen or more buckets.

"We need to take all of these with us," Levon said. He sealed the lid back in place with a tap of his fist.

"The drugs? Why?" Dale said. His stomach rumbled. He was already regretting his snack.

"This has to look like a robbery. A rival outfit. It'll have their bosses looking in all the wrong places for a while."

Dale stood blinking. He didn't like the idea but saw no other option.

"Start stacking them outside. I'm going to search the lab." Levon left Dale alone with the dead men.

Levon returned to the lab building. One man lay dead in an aisle between tables loaded down with tanks and tubes and the other equipment required to cook the mix that became crank. This had been the first man to die. Levon had found him working alone. Two shots to the back of the head while he bent over a laptop. Close up. No wild shots in this contained environment loaded with unstable chemical elements. The last thing Levon wanted was an explosion and, worse, a fire. He and Dale would need all the lead time they could get before this slaughter was discovered.

Holding his breath, he took a face mask from a hook off the wall and strapped it in place. It smelled like the breath of the last man to wear it. Onions and beer. It would keep the dangerous fumes in the air out of his lungs.

He worked quickly, pulling boxes, cartons and crates from the shelves before tossing them aside. His boots crunched on broken glass scattered everywhere on the concrete floor. At the rear of the lab was a steel cabinet locked with a padlock. There was a ring of keys on the belt of the man on the floor. One of them fit the padlock. Inside the cabinet he found what he was looking for.

Three canvas bags heavy with cash. All denominations of bills in thick rolls bound with rubber bands. Hard to tell how much was there. Mid six figures, he guessed from experience. His learning curve for rough estimating the value of bundles of currency had sharpened in recent months.

Levon hefted the bags and carried them outside. He found Dale bent over, puking up a stinking mess of Hydrox and beer. The plastic buckets were stacked.

"Back the truck up," Levon said. He tossed the key ring to his half-brother.

The buckets were loaded into the cargo area and back seat of the Kia. The rifles went atop them. The money bags rested on the console between them and on the floor at Dale's feet.

"It's going to be a long night," Levon said.

"We keeping this money?" Dale said. His arm rested atop a bag, the shoulder strap tight in his fist.

"I can't see why not."

"The drugs?"

"We'll find a place to dump them. Or bury them."

Levon piloted the Kia down the narrow jeep trail to where it joined the graveled fire road. He swung right to point them toward the county road.

"What about my truck? Can't leave it there. Can't move it either," Dale said.

"One thing at a time. The Walmart in Haley. Is it a twenty-four hour?" Levon said.

"Yeah."

"Then let's go."

They reached the county road and Levon turned left for Haley. Dale stared at the road ahead, the world of dark revealed only by the headlights stabbing into the night before them. He was surprised to find his hands weren't shaking. He was less surprised when he realized he'd been sweeping the shoulders of the road for possible IEDs while his half-brother drove.

*   *   *

"Are ya'll going to be all right?" Jessie Hamer said.

She looked from the kitchen to the family room where Merry had fallen asleep on the sofa watching a movie on TV. Sandy had covered her with a throw and headed off to bed an hour before.

"I hate to do this, Jessie. I really do. But Dale took me way out to God knows where and his damn truck broke down." Levon sounded contrite on the phone. She could hear the sounds of the woods at night behind his voice.

"Well, she's asleep now. I'd just as soon she spent the night here. I'll call Fern to let him know what's happening."

"Very kind of you."

"No trouble at all, Levon. Merry's been a joy to have over. Do you want me to send Fern out to where you are?"

"I wouldn't know how to tell him where we are. Somewhere in the woods above the water shed."

"All right. You get here when you can."

"Thanks so much, Jessie. I owe you."

They made their goodbyes and she replaced the phone in the charger.

19

The Walmart was a graveyard at two in the morning. They bought eight cans of Fix-a-Flat, a pair of flashlights, two gallons of bleach, a cube of car-cleaning rags and rubber gloves. They bought cheeseburgers and Cokes at a McDonald's drive through. They ate on the way back to Dale's truck. They passed two cars the whole way.

The headlights reflected yellow eyes near the bodies around Dale's truck. Foxes. Black shapes slinked away low to the ground into the greater dark.

The truck was as they left it. The ATVS also. Levon played a light over the scene. The foxes had gotten to the body of the cowboy. The soft tissue of his face was eaten away leaving behind white bone gleaming wet. The other two were undisturbed except for columns of ants.

Levon pumped the tires full while Dale cranked the engine to listen to the police scanner. A domestic disturbance in a trailer park. A single car accident near the high school. Levon tossed the empty aerosol cans into the truck bed. They both slipped on rubber gloves and wiped the borrowed rifles with rags soaked in bleach then tossed the guns near the bodies. Together they wiped down every surface inside and outside the Kia. They pulled off the gloves and stuffed them in the McDonald's bag along with the rest of their trash. They transferred the buckets of crystal and cash bags to the bed of Dale's truck.

"Your tires will last to get us home. Not much beyond that," Levon said.

"Can you come take me to the Goodyear tomorrow?" Dale said.

"Yeah. You have a place to stash those buckets?"

"I got a garage. I'll lock them in there."

"Take me on home. We'll get some sleep and finish this in the morning."

They got in the county truck. Dale did a three-point and aimed them back toward the county road through the woods. The sky was turning pink through the limbs above. Dale was so tired he felt boneless. His mouth and his eyes were dry and itchy. Everything seemed unreal and far away. Everything was fuzzy around the edges.

"Take a shower when you get home," Levon said.

"I know I stink," Dale said.

"We both do. It's not that. You need to get any residue off you. Wash all your clothes too. Better yet, burn them."

Dale nodded. He turned onto the county road. Cars came down the opposing lane, headlights casting watery light in the gray gloom. People driving to work in Colby, getting an early start on the day. They came to a stop behind a school bus flashing red lights where it was parked outside the entrance to a subdivision. A half dozen kids lined up to board. Women waiting with them, watching the bus take off. They all turned to walk back home, talking in pairs. No one spared a glance at the county truck following the yellow bus away toward town.

"Did we do the right thing here, Levon?" Dale said.

"We did the only thing," Levon said.

20

Danny Huff leaned back against the door of his state car to slip a pair of Tyvek booties over his brogans. He stood and adjusted his waistband to bring his holstered Colt revolver back to its accustomed place. He'd worn the big revolver so long there was a permanent indentation on his hip. He snapped his leather-clad badge onto his belt before flipping open a pair of Ray Bans from his shirt pocket. It was a warm one with summer almost here. He swept a hand through jet black hair and it came away damp with sweat. He left the suit jacket in the car.

He joined Ralph Durward on the gravel fire road. Durward had booties on over his trooper boots. The pink slip-ons contrasted with the trooper's immaculately pressed navy blue uniform and light blue tie. Other state cops and county deputies stood about among the vehicles waiting for further orders. There were state and local SUVs and cruisers along with a county coroner truck and a big forensics bus driven up from the Montgomery barracks overnight. They were arrayed along the verges of the forest road.

"Special Agent Huff," Danny said and extended his hand to Durward. "State Bureau is taking lead here and I lost the coin toss."

"Glad to have you here, sir," Durward said. He took Danny's hand in a strong dry grip. Blue eyes in a sun-creased face like tanned leather. A lifer, the man gave away nothing. If he was glad about giving up lead or angry right down to the ground Danny would never know.

"Have you been to the crime scene?" Danny said.

"I took a look. I can walk you through what we know and what we don't know," Durward said.

"Always good to know what you don't know," Danny said.

The trooper grunted a reply and led Danny past the other lawmen to where bands of yellow crime scene tape were stretched taut between trees across the opening of a dirt track. Durward held up the tape to allow Danny to duck under then followed.

They walked the track alone. It curved down into a deep holler, sheltering trees seeming to rise higher into the sky as they walked.

"Any sign of tire tracks?" Danny said. He gestured to the road surface of packed dirt.

"A heavy rain two nights ago washed away anything useful. There's depressions from a vehicle being parked closer into the buildings."

"Who found the bodies?"

"Kid down in one of the developments lost his dog. Family was up here hiking when the dog ran off. They came up this trail and ran across this site and called it in. County boys responded. Called us in right away."

"What about the other site?" Danny said.

"Found it when county boys went on a canvass for any campers or such might have seen or heard anything. Found the other three bodies and their all-terrains a couple miles uphill."

"How long they been there?"

"Rough estimate only? A week or more. Animals have been at them. Bugs and such. Wild dogs. Same thing at Site Two. I'd bet even money they all died around the same time."

"So, they ever find him?"

"Sir?"

"The dog. Did the family ever find the dog?" Danny said.

"No. They never did," Durward said.

* * *

Following his walk-around, Danny called in the forensics team. They parked their big ass bus as far along the trail as they dared bring it. An environmental clean-up team assigned by the county showed up as well. Danny had to settle a disagreement between them before it turned into a feud. The forensics nerds would deal with all of the crime scene except the lab building. They could have that when the tox crew finished their evaluation and cleared it for entry.

The two teams spread out across the three-building compound in their bunny suits. The tox crew wore hoods and breathers and entered the lab building with steel cases of gear. The forensics nerds established a grid search pattern and began poking their way across the assigned area.

"There's jack shit for me to do other than order them lunch," Danny said to Trooper Durward. "Can you show me to Site Two?"

"You sure you want to hike it, sir? It's rough ground," Durward said. He squinted at the steep slope rising behind the lab building.

"My grandparents on my mother's side were Cherokee. They used to tell me how a brave could run twenty miles up and down these hills without a break or a sip of water. Then run twenty miles back with a deer carcass slung over his back."

"So, we're hiking it, sir?" Durward said.

"Hell, no. You've got a four-wheel?" Danny said.

Durward nodded. Danny thought he saw a trace of a smile on the trooper's stone face.

"And it's air conditioned?"

"Like a meat locker, sir."

"Lead the way, my man," Danny said.

* * *

By evening it was Danny Huff's turn to play second banana.

Two federal agents arrived from the FBI's Nashville office. Agents Seffner and Greene needed a review of the twin mass murder scenes now determined to be a successful hijacking. It was down to Danny to bring them up to speed.

"A week to ten days ago this meth lab got hit presumably for product and cash. We'll know more when the med-ex report bounces back." Danny and the agents had taken shelter in the county forensics bus. They shared some not-horrible coffee and listened to the patter of fresh rain on the roof.

"Any idea if they got away with anything?" Agent Greene said. Or was it Seffner? They were both white guys in matching windbreakers and jock haircuts.

"No way to tell. The set-up suggests this lab was an earner. They had enough chems for a cook that could keep the whole state cranked up till New Years. There could have been a massive amount of the stuff here unless they'd already hauled it off."

"And cash?" Greene or Seffner asked.

"Again, no way to say. We don't know how this crew was set up. If the money came back this way or somewhere else. But given the number of bodies I'd say they were here guarding something. Cash or goods or both."

"Who were the dead guys?"

"Mexicans or like that? South of the border anyway. Covered in ink, most of them." Danny handed over his tablet. The agents scrolled through photos showing torsos, arms and legs covered in tattoos.

"Zetas," Greene or Seffner said.

"Cartel," Seffner or Greene said.

"We get migrants through here. Mostly stoop work at local farms in the south end of the county," Danny said. "Local deputies told me they've seen gang tags here and there for a year or so. But they had no idea they were up here cooking."

"Any ballistics back? What kind of firefight went on here?" one of the pair asked.

"One-sided. Site Two, the one up the hill? Buckshot and forty-five rounds. We found empty casings from the shooters only. The three dead men never got off a shot even though they were armed."

"And down at the lab?"

"More casings. Two-two threes. Chinese manufacture. The dead guys returned some fire but no sign they had any luck." Danny tipped a bit more creamer into his coffee to cut the bitterness.

"You have any crews locally could have pulled this off?"

"We have our meth labs, sure. They grew up when cooking crystal became more profitable than distilling feed corn. But nothing like a cartel deal. Dudes cooking in trailers and hunting cabins back in the woods. Small time."

"Another cartel then. A rivalry," Greene said to Seffner, or the other way around.

"Sinaloa. Guats. Or a wildcard outfit," perhaps Seffner said to Greene.

"So, this goes federal? Either you guys or DEA?" Danny said.

"We'll get back to you," one of the agents said.

"You'll be contacted with where to send all follow-up reports," said the other agent.

They stepped from the bus and into the rain never to be seen again.

21

Trey Wilkins wanted to be a cop more than anything else in the world.

A slight frame, fallen arches and the eyesight of a groundhog crushed those dreams. Still, he majored in law enforcement online at Liberty University. He was looking for any job that would put him close to the world of cops. Hell, he'd work a lunch wagon outside a Highway Patrol barracks if it's what he had to do to be close to the action.

When he found out that a few of the state police ballistics technicians were retiring he applied for the job. Almost a year went by and he got the call. His degree in police administration and his grades at Liberty recommended him. The state of Alabama sent him on an eight week course in firearms forensics then put him right to work studying lands and grooves on spent rounds recovered from crime scenes all over the state.

He was in hog heaven dealing with actual evidence, lethal evidence, recovered from the bodies of homicide victims. It wasn't slinging a gun and driving a cruiser but it was still being part of the game.

The collection of bagged and tagged rounds and casings recovered from sites One and Two (from a mass shooting incident designated ALEA #00978 Colby1 or Colby 2 5/24) was bewildering.

Almost two magazines worth of spent .223 rounds full metal jacket. .45 slugs. Some 7.62 X 39 rounds. And little baggies of buckshot which, from a ballistics study standpoint, were nearly useless. The empty shotgun cartridges found at the scene told Trey nothing. Deer rounds were common as dirt down in that county. The Walmart sold more shot rounds than anything else come the fall months each year.

Along with the crushed and malformed bullets came a collection of weapons found at both scenes. Semi-auto rifles. Handguns. No shotgun. No .45. Those must have belonged to the shooters.

Trey spent the time before lunch firing test rounds from each weapon into gel blocks for comparison to the various spent ammo. After lunch, he made the direct comparisons, scrolling through side-by-side shots of the magnified striations etched in each round by its passage through the barrels of the found weapons.

He squinted at the screen. Twiddled the mouse to impose one image over the other. He checked the reports coming along with the bagged evidence. One report, signed D. Huff, laid out the scenario of the mass shooting in something that read like a rough, artless short story.

"Something wrong there," Trey said to himself.

Danny Huff was treating Trooper Durward to barbecue at a roadside stand outside Colby. A black dude was making art at a big old tank-style grill on a trailer. Gray smoke drifting into the treetops to telegraph the promise of fulfilling every redneck's culinary desire for miles around. The dude's four kids served up the pulled pork in a killer sauce on soft rolls along with a big scoop of carrot and cabbage slaw. The two cops sat on the dropped tailgate of the trooper's state SUV, leaning forward to dig into the thick sandwiches so as not to drip the rich red goop on their clothes.

Danny's Galaxy thrummed in his pocket. He pulled it out to find a text loaded with images.

"I like your ringtone, Danny," Trooper Durward said. Johnny Cash. The opening three-part riff to "Folsom Prison Blues".

"Sweet Jesus on a seesaw," Danny said after a few moments taking in the text and grainy images.

"What is it?" the trooper said.

"The two-two-three slugs we picked out of the victims and walls at Site One? They came out of the ARs we found at Site Two."

"But your timeline has Site Two happening first. Makes no sense, sir." They were back on the clock. It was 'sir' now. Trooper Durward was all about old school discipline.

"What we have here is a fucking mystery," Danny said.

Gunny Leffertz said:
> *"Some folks won't listen to reason. Not even when reality is gnawing on their ass asking for seconds."*

22

It was a question Levon had anticipated long before it was asked.

"When can we spend some of the money?" Dale said.

Levon stepped away from the engine stand in Fern's barn and eyed Dale with a hard look. He had the manifold covers off the Mustang's engine preparatory to tearing the whole thing down. The trannie was already stripped to pieces on a work bench.

"What do you need money for?"

"I don't know. Mom's medications ain't cheap and my monthly check only goes so far." Dale shrugged. He lived with his mother in a double-wide on an acre or two the other side of the county road.

"I'll give you some money of my own. That do you?"

"What's the difference between your money and the money we took?"

"No one's looking for my money," Levon said. He dipped his hand into a can of gritty detergent. He worked the dollop in his hands, lifting grease from his skin.

"I don't think anyone's looking. Been near to a month now. Even the cops have forgotten about it. Bunch of dead Mexicans in the woods. No one gives a shit."

"Shows what you know." Levon walked out into the noonday sunlight and headed for the house. Dale followed.

In the kitchen, Uncle Fern was making a peanut butter and

banana sandwich while listening to Rush Limbaugh on a radio set on the counter.

"Want a sandwich?" Fern said to the men entering through the screen door. "I can brew some fresh coffee."

"Dale isn't staying," Levon said. He headed up the stairs for his room.

Dale took a seat at the kitchen table to wait.

"How's your mother doing?" Fern asked, setting a plate down on the table and seating himself. There was a glass and a carton of milk.

"Okay, I guess. Just telling Levon. She's on blood thinners and shit still and the Medicare's only so much help."

Uncle Fern let out a snort.

"Damn doctors. They tell us to take pills but not how to pay for them. Clinic in Haley wanted me on those cholesterol drugs. I told 'em I'd just switch to drinkin' blue john." Fern poured himself a glass of skim milk from the carton.

Levon came back into the kitchen. He slapped down a wad of bills on the table in front of Dale.

"What I owed you for that favor," he said.

"Sure. Sure. All good," Dale said. He stood to pocket the wad. A glance told him it was a half inch thick stack of fifties.

"I'll walk you out," Levon said. He held the screen door for his half-brother.

"Fern know what we done?" Dale said when they were away from the house.

"He only knows we were up to something. And he knows that what he's ignorant of he can't tell no one about."

"You really think someone's looking for what we took?"

"These guys aren't like cops. They don't need evidence. They'll move on a suspicion. You start spending big and draw attention to yourself? Step out of cover once. All it takes."

"Sounds like you don't trust me to have any common sense, Goose," Dale said. He opened the door of his truck and stood leaning in the opening.

"Those tires. What they cost you?" Levon nodded to the four new Michelins with chrome rims highlighted in electric blue.

"That's on me. I had some put aside," Dale said. He tapped his pocket with his fingers.

"Don't ask for more. You wait till I tell you it's all good."

"Shit, Goose. It was for my mother."

"She's not *my* mother, Dale."

Levon walked back to the house. Dale raised rooster tails of dust peeling off Fern's lot.

23

"Interdepartmental cooperation my ass," Laura Strand said.

"No luck with our brothers and sisters in the intelligence community?" Nancy Valdez said.

Their daily morning briefing started all wrong.

The coffee station on their floor was out of creamer. So Laura wasn't happy.

It was Tony Marcoon's turn to bring the donuts. There were three with peanut sprinkles and Chad had a severe peanut allergy. So Chad Bengstrom wasn't happy.

They were coming up on the deadline for their second review with Brett Sylvester in three days and had jack shit to show him. Nancy was deeply unhappy.

Tony liked his coffee black. Could eat his fill of donuts without fear of anaphylactic shock or gaining an ounce. And departmental reviews were speed bumps on the highway of life. So Tony was not happy but not unhappy.

"NSA. Navy Intelligence. CIA. Dickheads all of them," Laura said and slapped her child-sized hand down atop a stack of folders tinted in shades of teal, lime green and gray.

It had the makings of a rant so the others remained quiet.

"Levon Cade was inducted into the Marines at eighteen. Went through boot camp at Parris Island then special weapons training at Pendleton. Typical career path for an eager young jarhead, right? Then it all goes dark," Laura said.

"Redactions. Redactions. And more redactions. The only text remaining between the bars of black tell us he was deployed to Iraq, Afghanistan, the Philippines and Colombia. We can guess he was at the Western Hemisphere Institute down there. A spook unit for hunting narcos. But who knows? Was he part of a deep cover hunter/killer team? Bodyguarding dignitaries? They know and won't tell us.

"Then, all of a sudden, he's back in Huntsville living like Joe Sixpack. He's married. Has a kid. Gets a prescription for Xanax from the VA for post-trauma. Just another returning vet. Works dead-end jobs, entry level stuff. Security guard. Delivery truck driver. Never stays anywhere long. And between jobs he's gone like a ghost."

"The theory was he was still active with whatever agency was deploying him before," Nancy said. She sipped black coffee and winced.

"And that's all it is. A theory," Laura said. "I dug into the Cade family financials. They lived within their means. A mortgage. Car loans. No sign of hidden income streams. She worked as a substitute teacher. He did his blue collar thing. It all looked like they were living off their salaries."

"The American dream," Chad said. He eyed the remaining donuts with a mix of desire and dread.

"Until his wife was diagnosed with cancer," Laura said. "Combined bill for treatment up to the time of her death was well over a million dollars. Paid in full right after her funeral."

"Her parents helped with that, right? Her father's a surgeon?" Nancy said.

"I looked into their returns, too. The Roths did not show a payout to any of the hospitals or clinics that treated Arlene Cade. Not a penny. Someone covered the costs and it wasn't them." Laura reached out to pluck a cream-filled from the box.

"Three days, people," Nancy said. "Three days and we have to show something to Brett to justify our work here."

Laura munched her donut with a pensive expression. Chad looked at his open laptop sullenly. Nancy sighed.

"Well, I have something," Tony said. He flipped open a notepad.

The others turned to him. Nancy spread her hands to welcome the former homicide cop's revelation.

"The Roths. What happened to them?" Tony said. "Levon Cade first comes on the radar when he's a person of interest in the death of his in-laws. Marcia Roth is found dead, shot through the head in their house which is burnt to the ground in a clear case of arson. Dr. Jordan Roth is never seen again. Cade was involved in a wicked custody battle over his daughter Meredith."

"Cade was cleared," Chad said. "He was hours away at the time of the murder and fire. Time-stamped video at a fast food drive-through."

"That's not where I'm going," Tony said. "I'm looking at the father-in-law. He's suspect number one in his wife's murder. But nothing feels right about it. What's the motive? Where'd he get the gun? There's no record of a purchase or registration. And a single gunshot to the back of the head is not your typical crime of passion."

"Not seeing how any of this leads us to Cade," Laura said.

"I think it's worth exploring because of all the other shit happening at the time." Tony flipped to a new page. "Cade was working security for Robert Joseph Wiley who owned a construction firm in Huntsville. Wiley's daughter was abducted down in Tampa. Her body turns up in a swamp down there."

"You're reaching, Tony," Nancy said. "The Bureau guys looked into it."

"The feebs know fuck-all about homicide investigations." Tony snorted. He wanted to wrap this up. He needed a cigarette after his coffee. "The girl's body is identified and a couple of jerk-off bikers are nailed for it. But they say they only buried her as a favor for someone. They flip on these Russians and get some slack on their sentences. Only, guess what, the Russians they flip on are all dead."

The others sat forward.

"In fact lots of Russians are dead over a two week period before the Wiley girl's body is found. The Tampa cops are finding them all over the bay area. Somewhere in there Marcia Roth is shot dead and her house is torched and her husband disappears. At the same time Levon Cade is in the wind and off the grid with his daughter only to pop up on the radar a year later in Maine."

"And more dead career criminals," Nancy said.

"Then a psycho road trip across the Rust Belt wasting felons along the way," Chad said.

"Forget about that," Tony said. "Look back at the situation with Cade and the missing girl."

"What situation?" Nancy said.

"Cade's boss at Wiley and Manners can't find his daughter. I pulled the missing persons reports. No action from Tampa PD. He's frustrated. His little girl's missing and nobody seems to care. He sends this badass on his security payroll down to check things out."

"With no idea who Cade really is." Chad was nodding and smiling.

"Exactly. And Cade turns it all into a total clusterfuck," Tony said. "Pissing off a shitload of Russians."

"Who send someone to Huntsville to find him," Laura said.

"Who turn up the in-laws," Tony said.

"And they stop there? Kill the Roths then forget about it?" Chad said.

"And I don't think they killed Dr. Jordan Roth," Tony said. The table went silent as he came to his punchline.

24

Merry's face was set hard, her back straight and grip easy on the reins. She matched the rhythm of the horse trotting easy around the broad ring. A press of her right knee set the horse on a course away from the fence line. It amazed her each time it happened. This enormous animal responding to the touch of her leg.

"You ready to give it some gas?" Sandy called. She leaned back on a wooden jump set in the center of the ring.

"Yeah!" Merry said. The quarter horse's ears flicked back at her voice. Merry pressed her heels against the flanks. The horse sped to a canter. Merry fought the urge to hold the reins tighter. She kept the clutch of her legs firm but not clenched. As she adjusted to the faster pace the ride became smoother, rider and mount moving as one. A feeling welled up from inside. She had no words for it. A simple joy. A sense of accomplishment. It was more than that.

A moment of perfection.

"She's really taken to it," Jessie said. She and Levon stood in the grass of the paddock watching Merry ride the ring. Close enough to see her but not enough to distract.

"All little girls love horses," Levon said.

"They like the *idea* of horses," Jessie said. "But your girl loves every single thing about them. She's been coming here for what? A month or more? Always ready to help with even the dirtiest chores. Most kids get bored."

"She does sit well."

Jessie turned to him.

"'Sit well?' I never saw you ride and now you're an expert."

"Army taught me to ride."

"I thought you were in the Marines," she said. Her crooked smile and a tilt of the head.

"I'm going to step away. I don't want Merry to know I'm watching," Levon said.

They walked together into the shade of some dogwoods. There was a sagging picnic table covered in white petals from the blooming branches above. Jessie took a seat at the end of a bench.

"She's asking me to buy her a horse," he said. He leaned back on the table, eyes still on the ring as Merry reined to a stop.

"Not just any horse. That horse. The one she's on. Belongs to one of my boarders and he's looking to sell," Jessie said.

"I don't know."

"You have a barn."

"My uncle has a barn. I don't own anything but my car and our clothes."

"It's not the horse. You don't plan on staying."

"I don't know what I plan, Jessie."

"Merry hasn't said much. But I know from what she *has* said you two have moved around a lot. I know she hasn't been in school."

"I do what I can. She does lessons."

"Not the same as a home, Levon."

He said nothing. His eyes were on Merry leading the horse from the ring while Sandy held the gate open. They were laughing. He could see their smiles.

"I don't mean to sound like I'm her mother," Jessie said.

"You make a good mother," he said. He shifted his gaze to her. Jessie's face reddened.

"If I didn't know better I'd say that was a compliment," she said.

"None higher," he said. He pushed off from the table and offered his hand to help her stand.

"Now, are you going to tell me about why the Army taught you to ride?" Jessie said. They were walking to the stable together, following the girls leading the horse.

"I'll tell you some of it," Levon said.

Sandy lounged back on a stack of feed bags to watch Merry cool down the quarter horse. The spaniel leapt up to lay down beside her, driving his head under her fingers for a pet.

"Water warm enough?" she said.

"I tested it on my arm," Merry said. She played the hose over the animal's back. The flesh along his ribs trembled as the lukewarm water trickled down his flanks.

"Too cold and Bravo's muscles cramp."

"I know, I know." Merry ran a steel comb over the hair followed by water from the hose. The dried sweat and dust came away from the hair. The water turned muddy ochre in a puddle pooled around a drain in the floor. She washed down the legs, ducking under the cross-ties to rub handfuls of water on the horse's brow. Bravo playfully nudged her with his muzzle.

"Your dad is here," Sandy said. She lay back with her head on crossed arms, one leg over the other. The spaniel jumped down to the floor to lap water.

"I didn't see him," Merry said. She squirted Bravo's legs with fly repellent from a spray bottle.

"Him and my mom were watching you in the ring."

"Uh huh."

"I think my mom likes your dad. I mean, really likes him. They used to be boyfriend-girlfriend, you know?"

"He told me something about it." Merry's brow wrinkled as she sprayed some fly stuff on her hand and rubbed it on Bravo's twitching ears.

"Long time ago."

Merry unhooked the cross-ties. She led Bravo back toward his stall. Sandy hopped off her chaise of feed bags to follow.

"Your dad's a serious guy. Kind of scary."

"Scary?" Merry said.

"In a sexy way." Sandy shrugged.

Merry giggled. The skein of freckles across her nose darkened.

25

Beto asked his uncle for a gunfighter. A real badass hombre, a *sicario* out of Matamoros or Saltillo.

Instead his *tio* Fausto sent him Sabio.

Now Beto and his brother Memo had to cart around this *viejo* with his big choppy sideburns, gray as ash. He looked like an elderly Mexican Elvis impersonator. Even worse, Sabio insisted Beto drive him around Colby in a piece of shit Dodge Ram instead of Beto's shit-hot Lexus RX. And even worse still, the Ram had a single bench seat so Beto had to drive around with the old man crammed between him and Memo. They looked like a trio of wetbacks running an errand for some gringo contractor.

But Sabio was *jefe*. And this was not Beto's *plaza*. So Beto shut his mouth and concealed his impatience.

"Obey Sabio's word as if it were my own," *tio* Fausto said over the phone from Coahuila. "They do not call him 'Sabio' without good reason."

Sabio. Wise one.

"But we have been fucked in the ass, *tio*," Beto said. "Cousin Lalo and his crew are dead. The rock and our money is gone."

"Whose money?" Fausto said. There was still a smile to be heard in his voice. But Beto had seen that smile dry up like rain on a summer sidewalk.

"Your money, *tio*," Beto said.

"You still have two labs going. Money is money. More comes every day."

"But this is a matter of *honor*."

"You are still young, Beto. You have very simple ideas about honor. You confuse honor with pride. It is a mistake of the young."

Beto was swallowing a lot of pride now. He was thirty-two and yet his uncle still thought of him as a kid.

"This is a matter of business," Fausto continued. "If we have rivals, they must be dealt with. Show Sabio all over your *plaza*. Let him see what the big picture is like. Let him decide what is best to do."

And so, Beto spent week after week driving Sabio all over the county to play detective. Beto wanted to give him a rundown of the crime structure in the county. He knew of only a few of the names of the *gabacho* operators. Some who ran stills. Some who were cooking meth. A few bringing in heroin and oxy. Where a couple of pot farms were hidden. These rednecks were a secretive bunch to strangers. It came from generations of eluding federal cops. Beto could relate. It was the same down in Mexico.

The difference was the topography. The ridges and valleys cut across the north end of the county leaving a lot of the *gabacho* operations deep in inaccessible hollers like the canyons in Chihuahua. Those valleys held their secrets like graves.

Beto was all for striking out at the redneck meth labs he already knew about. Send a message. Take their money. Leave *their* cousins dead.

"*Incluso el tigre caza huele el suelo*," Sabio said in his sleepy voice.

Even the tiger smells the ground when he hunts.

What the fuck did that mean? Beto wanted to ask him.

Instead he nodded at the old man's sage wisdom and drove him around to any place where *campesinos* could be found. Beto had to endure hours in the truck listening to long conversations between his brother and Sabio.

Memo was a fat moron that Beto's mother made him promise to look out for all his days on earth. He made the promise on her deathbed when she was going through the chemo and he was only a little boy. He was a grown man now and his mother's cancer treatments worked and she was still alive down in Durango with his stepfather.

"But a promise is a promise," she would remind Beto on the phone each time he bitched about some stupid thing his *idiota hermano* had done.

Now he drove around in a crappy pickup while his little brother had "deep" conversations with Sabio like some retard Luke Skywalker talking to a drowsy Obi Wan. Only deep drags of Tamaulipas skunk kept him from driving the Ram into a utility pole sometimes.

They went to fields and orchards to talk to pickers and packers. The Marriott and Motel 8 in Haley to talk to maids. Tire garages and oil changing places to talk to mechanics. The landfill to talk to drivers. Gated communities to the south and north to talk to lawn care workers. And every *un congal* where whores worked out of trailers to service lonely peons missing a taste of home and horny gringos with a taste for wetback pussy. Early mornings sitting outside the Home Depot and the garden center talking to pick-up workers waiting for day labor jobs.

The peons Sabio talked to had no reason to answer the questions of some nosy old man. But one look at his companions, two young guys in snakeskin boots and rodeo shirts untucked, turned every *pinche mojado* into a willing font of information. The illegal labor force in the county was an invisible network of informants. They saw all while remaining unseen.

Sabio never shared what he learned. He never wrote anything down. It was impossible to tell from the *viejo's* demeanor if he was making any progress at all in finding out who stole the *plaza's* drugs and money. He always wore the same half-lidded expression, always spoke in the same sotto voce, rhythmic and hypnotic yet insistent.

Two weeks of their learning tour was wearing on Beto. He wanted to punish someone. He could appreciate the wisdom of taking the time to make certain they killed the correct person. Still, he felt it was long past time that someone, *anyone*, suffered for the death of his cousins Lalo, Pepe and the others. Not that he gave a shit about his cousins who were dumb enough to let some *pinche* hillbillies sneak up on them. But the theft of so much product and cash made him, Beto, look like a fool.

Yeah, it was about pride. Why not? Was his pride not worth something?

They were parked at the Creamee-Freez. Sabio wanted soft-serve. Memo sat on the tailgate licking sprinkles from a cone and swinging his legs like a child. Sabio leaned on the hood with his own cone, looking into the sky as though he might find answers in the clouds. Beto was lactose intolerant and so stood watching traffic and picking at a bag of ranch chips.

"When are we going to *move*, Sabio? Any clue or are you going to play Colombo forever?" Beto asked.

"*Que tan rapido crecer el cabello de un hombre?*" Sabio said, his tongue white with ice cream.

How fast does a man's hair grow?

Beto remained silent, munching chips with renewed fury.

26

"They're building a mosque over in Teeter," Melvin said close to the heavyset man's ear.

"Yeah?" Delbert said.

"Oh yeah. A mosque. Big old barn of a place," Melvin said. He was practically shouting over the buzz of shears he was running around the back and sides of his customer's head.

He was also speaking to the other three men seated in the sagging leather chairs lined against a wall across from the barber chairs. One of them was actually waiting for a haircut. The others were a pair who only stopped by E&B Barbers to watch Melvin's cable. The pair nodded at the barber's remarks but their full attention was on the TV mounted on a high shelf. A lady judge was hectoring a pair of sad sacks from a bench while the audience laughed. She banged her gavel for order and they laughed more.

"What in hell do they need a damned mosque for? I been to Teeter more times than I can say and never once saw an Arab," Melvin said.

Delbert's dyed-dark hair fell in a blizzard from the whirring blades, revealing silver roots. A haircut these days put twenty years on him. Come in with wavy auburn locks, thanks to Clairol, and come out an old man. Never mind, Beth-Ann would give him a rinse tonight. Make Old Man Time back away a step or two.

"Hell, they were always a different bunch over there in Teeter," Delbert said.

"There is that," Melvin said. "Hot towel?"

"You know it," Delbert said. The hot towel was what he looked forward to most. And the razor shave afterwards. Mostly because

Melvin stopped talking during that portion of the grooming process.

He closed his eyes and felt the barber jacking him back into a reclining position. The embrace of the towel cut him off from the world for a few welcome moments. His face covered but for his mouth, he felt the heat from the steaming cloth seep into his face to unwind his whole body.

Running over the details of today's calendar in his mind. And it was all in Delbert's mind. Nothing written down. No damn smart phones. No phones of any kind. He did his business in person, face to face, so as to see the other man's eyes. Just like his daddy and his daddy before him.

Following his haircut he'd have Howard drive him back home for lunch. Most of his crew weren't even out of bed much before noon and barely sober before dark again. Afternoon was the best time for his rounds. It was Tuesday and that was collection day. Howard would drive him up Cumberland and hook west across the county visiting hollers and remote farms to take his piece of the business being done there.

He hoped he wouldn't have trouble with Clay Johnson again this week. The man did not understand the concept of quotas. He had Howard break Clay's jaw last year, but the lesson didn't take. The dumb son-bitch came up two hundred dollars short and thought he'd make up for it with promises.

"I can't spend promises," Delbert told him.

"Things was off last week," Clay said.

"Really? I watch the news every day and I didn't see anything about all the potheads suddenly not wanting to get high," Delbert said. "Did Jesus come down and clean alla their asses up?"

Delbert made some promises of his own. Clay would either make good this week plus a two hundred dollar bonus or pay in collateral. And the only collateral Clay had was four daughters.

He used to have five but Delbert took one in payment during Clay's default last year. The girl earned for Delbert out of a trailer until he sold her on to a guy from Memphis. Sweet girl. Ugly as sin.

The towel came off and Delbert felt Melvin's fingers gently applying warm creamy lather to his cheeks and throat. The keen edge of the razor followed to glide over his face leaving only baby-smooth flesh behind.

Out on the street Delbert kicked the door of the Escalade. Howard woke sudden where he'd dozed off behind the wheel. He looked at Delbert with an apologetic simper. His big fat face looked childish in contrition.

"You do know you're supposed to watch my ass, little brother," Delbert said. He took his seat on the passenger side. The Escalade felt chilly after the crushing humidity outside. The dash dinged until he'd shut the door and belted in.

"Sorry, Del," Howard said. He snapped on the wipers to remove the condensation from the windshield.

"Take us home," Delbert said. "Get a grilled cheese and a Coke then hit the road on our route."

The dogs didn't come out to greet him.

Beth-Ann's schnauzer always came barreling out through the doggie door at the first sound of tires on the drive. His big old Irish wolfhound would be loping after the yapping terrier, snout up and baying.

Delbert's vintage pickup and Beth-Ann's BMW were in the circular turnaround in the shade of the spreading willow. He climbed out and raced up the steps to the sun porch. Behind him he heard a stuttering clicking noise. He turned to see Howard tumbling from the cab of the Escalade. Some skinny dude was riding Howard's bulk to the ground, a stun gun pressed to the big man's neck.

A boot sole on the floorboards of the porch behind him.

A flash of blinding blue light filled his field of vision before everything swirled away.

27

"Things just got officially fucked up," Danny Huff said. It was a general announcement to the state highway cops and county forensics geeks working around him on the road surface.

"Yes, sir," Trooper Durward said.

County and state cars were parked along the shoulder of the road, lights twirling. Cruisers blocked the road leaving a traffic-free mile of backwoods switchback exclusive to investigators. The road ran generally north-south through deep woods following the floor of a holler and connecting a township and county road. Only a few properties along the little used way. Marked with rusted mailboxes, the houses were invisible at the ends of unpaved driveways running far back into the trees. Not a much traveled road. The body had been found by a driver heading to work a morning shift at the Home Depot in Haley.

The state bureau agent and the trooper stood in booties watching the bustle of an evidence team photographing, measuring and searching the cracked asphalt for more things to photograph and measure. They moved along, dropping yellow wedge markers behind them like bunny-suited Hansels and Gretels. They were following a trail of drying blood running parallel with the dotted white line in the middle of the road. The trail was thick in places, thin in others, and finally dribbled away to a series of blobs in shrinking sizes over almost a half-mile of road surface.

"What will come of all this? Other than long hours and a shit-pile of reports?" Danny said. He flicked a ghostly white moth from his sleeve.

"Nothing good, sir," Durward said. He stood stolid with thumbs hooked in his gun belt.

"Hey, Danny. You still lead on this?" A county forensics tech walked up to Danny.

"I am that place where the shit gathers, Elliott," Danny said.

"It is a close one. Damn this humidity." Elliott Crabb took the fingers of his vinyl gloves in his fingers and popped them off. He pulled the zipper of his bunny suit down to reveal a t-shirt sodden with sweat. He removed a tissue from somewhere inside the suit and wiped the condensation from his glasses.

"I think we'd all appreciate it if atrocities like this were committed on more clement days," Danny said. A wince more than a smile.

"What we have is a white male. Middle-aged. Naked. Bound by the wrists. Up this way." Elliott pointed north to where the road curved away around a rock face jutting off the sloping ground.

"We know who he is?"

"He's printed. We're waiting to hear back."

"Cause of death?"

"Blood loss. Bled out."

"Shot? Stabbed?" Danny said.

"It's more complicated. Up there is most of the victim." Elliott nodded north then pointed south. "His tackle is down there."

"You mean he was castrated?"

"After a fashion."

"You gonna make me beg, Elliott?"

"It's only an idea, mind you. But I think he was being dragged behind a vehicle with some kind of line tied around his genitals. A rope or cable. Somewhere back where the body lies the man and his special purpose became separated."

"Jesus almighty." Danny eyed the trail of blood droplets spattered on the white line with a fresh understanding. He imagined the unknown man, hands bound behind him, running on bare feet to keep up. Finally falling or simply unable to keep pace. The line going taut.

"We found where the bits came loose from whatever brand of knot that secured them. Lucky for us no coyotes or buzzards came along to carry them off."

"Any evidence of the vehicle?"

"There's a partial tire track in a smear of blood. We might be able to work with that if it's enough to identify the make."

A vamp of music sounded from a pocket of Elliott's bunny suit. *Hawaii Five-O* theme. He pulled out a smart phone and eyed the screen.

"Got I.D. from the victim's prints," Elliott said.

"Let me see," Danny said. He motioned for the phone.

Multiple mug shots of a chunky, pasty looking guy with uncombed hair wearing an insolent smile for the camera. A list of felonies going back thirty years. Assaults. DUIs. Possession, manufacture and distribution of unlicensed alcohol. Possession of cocaine and other controlled substances. Manslaughter. Car theft. Criminal conspiracy. A few convictions led to time at Draper and Holman.

"Delbert Mathers," Danny said.

"I've heard of him, sir," Trooper Durward said.

"Me too. Not recently. I'm sure that's not due to clean living or Delbert's discretion though." Danny scrolled down. No arrests in the past eight years.

Danny handed over his Galaxy to Elliott Crabb.

"Do what you need to do to get all that on my dingus here," Danny said.

Elliott tabbed away at his own phone to move the pertinent data to the agent's device. The Tennessee Three ringtone came strumming on Danny's phone. Elliott handed it back.

"Let's walk the scene, shall we?" Danny said. "Then I'll work up a list of people who might have hated this son-bitch enough to go to all this trouble."

Together they walked around the curve of the road, staying well clear of the yellow markers, to where the body of the late Delbert Mathers lay in a lake of his own blood. Flies swarmed over the ivory pale flesh and at the edges of the drying spill. Elliott led them south along the crimson trail to where a sad lump of tissue and sinew rested on the asphalt like some obscene afterthought. A female forensics geek crouched over the mess trying to lift it with tongs into an insulated container.

Danny was startled from the morbid hypnosis of the scene before him by the sound of his phone.

It was county dispatch.

"I was told this may be of interest to you, sir," the dispatcher said.

A second possible multiple homicide scene less than four miles from where Danny and the trooper stood. As the crow flies. A forty-five minute drive on coiled snake roads. A property belonging to a family named Mathers.

"Looks like our day's just getting started, Ralph," Danny said.

Gunny Leffertz said:
"Feel that? The air going still all around? It's life taking a deep breath just before it shits all over you."

28

Levon's sat phone buzzed atop the workbench. He'd just pulled a piston assembly from an oil bath. He wiped the worst of the grease from his hands to pick up.

The readout told him it was Dale's cell. He tabbed the answer key and put the phone to his ear. He didn't speak.

He and Dale had left it raw the last time they spoke. Levon was not in a mood to apologize. He waited for Dale to open the conversation.

Only a hissing from the other end. Under the hiss a murmur of voices. No sound of breathing. Someone touched Levon's number and was now speaking to someone else. He couldn't pick out words, only sounds. Enough to know neither of the speakers was Dale. And both spoke a language that was not English.

Uncle Fern woke where he slept in his recliner, a book open on his knee. Levon was into his gun cabinet, selecting a bolt action with a scope and lever action.

"There something you need to tell me, nephew?" Fern said. He levered the Lazy Boy upright.

"Not sure. Stay in the house. Keep a shotgun handy. Bring in the dogs." Levon picked up two boxes of shells and headed for the kitchen.

"Where you off to?" Fern said.

"Dale's," Levon said. He was through the screen door and out toward his truck.

Levon left the 4Runner parked by the wall of the floodgate at the foot of Dale's holler.

He trotted into the trees and followed a familiar deer trail that climbed the slope and followed along the face of the hill. It was a place he knew well from back in the day when he and Dale played Indians in these woods. Their tribe was made up of local boys. They would stalk game and hunt imaginary enemies. The game would almost always end with Levon and Dale fighting for who would be chief of the war party.

The narrow path jinked around rocks and exposed roots in a lazy circle that hugged the incline all the way to a place above Dale's double-wide and car barn. Levon squatted in a spot where he could see down to the two buildings set apart on opposite sides of a clearing.

He unlimbered the Remington 700 from his shoulder to fix his eye to the scope. He swept the lens over the property. Dale's former county truck sat before the house. A second vehicle, a newer Camaro, was pulled up to the car barn.

Levon made his way down the slope under the shelter of the trees. He was careful not to snag branches on the barrel of the rifle slung over his shoulder. He moved silent past the scorched ground of Dale's trash burn pile. He used the cover of a rusting lawn shed he kept between him and the rear of the house.

He set down the rifle on the grass. His .45 in his hand, Levon levered the screen door open into a combination mudroom and laundry. A fat woman in terry cloth slippers and a house dress was down before an open clothes dryer. She lay atop a heap of laundry dyed crimson from multiple stab wounds to her throat. A spray of blood climbed the wall to dot the ceiling tiles.

Dale's mom.

Levon stepped around the body, avoiding the still tacky spread of blood on the tiles. He slipped past a utility room where the central air hummed and into the kitchen.

A man sat at the kitchen table eating ice cream from a gallon tub. An owlish looking man with dark skin and broad white sideburns. The man's eyes widened as he took in the big gringo approaching from around the Frigidaire. The man's hand went to the pistol lying on the table.

Levon's first shot took the old man through the head. The second punched through his throat as the chair tipped over under him.

The man lay on his back with one remaining eye still staring. The spoon clenched in his dead hand. His lips smeared white with melting ice cream.

Levon was moving fast through the double-wide, .45 held close in a two-hand grip. The front sights shifting with his line of sight. He cleared the six rooms within the house in seconds. The man in the kitchen was alone in the house.

The lot outside remained quiet but for the chirrup of birds. The two parked vehicles were empty. No shadows moved inside the car barn.

He returned to the laundry room and exited past the body of Dale's mother. The .45 went back into the clamp holster at his back. The Remington in his fists, he moved around the side of the house. Using the vehicles in the yard for cover, Levon approached the car barn with the rifle tight in his shoulder at a fast walk.

Dale was alone in the car barn. He sat on the floor secured to the leg of a work bench with tie wraps around his wrists and neck. Balls naked. Face raw and bleeding from blunt trauma. An oily rag shoved in his mouth. He was a map of bruises with a serious third degree burn to the toes and sole of one foot. The flesh was black, powdered with dead white tissue. The whole leg to the knee was angry red and swelling with fluid.

Levon swept the interior to make certain they were alone. He cut the tie wraps with a clasp knife before pulling the rag from Dale's mouth.

"Shit, Goose. Shit." Dale was panting. Hyperventilating.

"Where are they, Dale?" Levon said.

"I don't know. I don't know."

"How many?" Levon cuffed Dale's face to keep him conscious, focused.

"Three. Two young fuckers and an old man."

"Elvis sideburns?"

"Uh huh."

"He's dead, Dale."

"Good. Good. Fucker talked on a cell phone the whole time the other two were working on me."

"What did you tell them?"

Dale turned away. His eyes searching the floor as if the answers to Levon's question lay there.

Levon grasped his chin and pulled Dale's face upright.

"What did you tell them?" Levon pressed his grip harder.

"Sorry. So sorry, brother." Dale's eyes welled up. His face turned red under the bruises.

"My name? Uncle Fern's name?"

Dale nodded, his eyelids crushed together.

"Get up. Get your ass up." Levon hooked an arm under Dale's elbow and yanked him to his feet. Dale cried out when his scorched sole touched the floor. He stood hobbling on his good foot. He bit his lip against the pain as Levon helped him to the county truck.

"You're going to drive to Fern's. Tell him to fort up." Levon helped Dale get seated in the truck.

"But I'm bare-assed, Goose." Dale whined like back when they were kids and Levon won whatever game they were playing. Again.

"Nothing your uncle ain't seen before." Levon belted him in. He handed him the rifle through the window.

"What about my mama?"

"She's dead. Sorry."

"I ain't sure I can drive," Dale said. He sat angled on the seat to position his left leg over the pedals.

"I'm not staying here, Dale. If you want to wait here for those guys to come back then that's up to you."

Dale gunned the truck away in a spray of gravel.

Levon ran down the drive to the road then down to the floodgate. He picked up the sat phone from the seat of the truck. First he called Fern to tell him to look out for Dale. He hung up while the old man was still firing questions at him. He keyed in Jessie's number. She picked up on the third ring.

"Where are you, Jessie?" He kept his voice level.

"I'm on a farm call up to Lewton. The funniest—"

He cut off her story. "Is Merry with you?"

"Yes. She wanted to come along. I hope it's all right."

"It is. It's great. Can you keep her away from Fern's until I call you?"

"I guess so. Sure. Is something wrong?"

"All I want is for you to keep Merry with you and not bring her back here till I tell you it's all right."

"I can do that, Levon. Can you tell me—"

He broke the connection, tossed the sat phone to the seat beside him, and brought the Toyota to life. He swung out onto the two-lane in a sharp loop in time to meet a big pickup coming around the curve. The truck hit him broadside and, joined in a T-bone, they careened off the road down into a brush-choked ditch.

Levon was thrown flying from behind the wheel and airborne across the cab. He slammed his back against the far door.

Glass exploded. He struck his head hard on the jamb.

Dazed, he rolled to drop into the narrow gap between the seat and dash.

A shadow filled the broken window above him. An arm reached in, spilling glass. Voices, emphatic, from outside.

A hand stretched toward him holding a quivering blue light. His head struck hard on the door.

Burning. Then numbness.

Then nothing.

29

"This is some sick shit," Danny Huff said.

He said it as much to the world as to Trooper Durward and the gathered army of law enforcement in Delbert Mathers' big-ass great room.

A lot of years as a highway cop, homicide cop and state bureau agent exposed Danny Huff to some bad stuff. There were things he wish he could unsee. Stuff that could rouse him from a deep sleep. Not nightmares or even dreams; more like unbidden memories refusing to stay put in his past.

That time he was first on scene when a bus carrying a youth choir back from Charleston got in the path of a semi that crossed the median. The time he answered a complaint of children screaming to find a mother sitting on the toilet reading a magazine with her three drowned children lying lined up by the bathtub in a neat row. The traffic stop turning into a gunfight leaving his partner dead on the street and Danny covered in the blood and brains of a driver committed to going out in battle with John Law.

But nothing like this. Nothing close to this. Nothing in the same universe as this.

The castle of Delbert Mathers' hillbilly fiefdom was a sprawling rancher centered around a two-story tall great room. Looked like the waiting room of a Smoky Mountain resort.

Now it took on the appearance and smell of an abattoir. The only difference being that cattle and swine died quick merciful deaths at the blow of an air hammer between their eyes.

These people died slow. And scared. That much was clear.

They were slung up by their heels from the main exposed

beam high up on the ceiling. A thick, load bearing joist that could take the strain of near a half ton of additional weight on it.

Two men. Big old boys raised on biscuits and gravy. Two women. One slim. The other more on the porky side.

Someone had gone at them with some kind of blade. An ax. A machete. Something that was swung with furious intent to chop away fingers, limbs, noses, ears. Beneath the hanging forms was an untidy heap of parts staining the woven rug below. White bone. Pink muscle. Yellow fat.

Worse than anything else was the sight of cording used as tourniquets to tie off legs and arms above the cuts. Some sick bastards—Danny couldn't see how this was the work of one actor—tying off the arms and legs to slow bleeding. They wanted their victims to last.

Danny stepped outside to breathe in something cleaner. It wasn't enough. He bummed a Marlboro off one of the forensics techs unloading the bus.

Once a two pack a day man, he'd quit smoking when he left the homicide division for the state bureau. Back when every day meant snooping around a murder scene, a long pull from a cigarette was a welcome change from the stench of blood, shit and piss that came along with the job. Some bodies got ripe enough to make him burn his clothes. No way to get the stink out. He'd shower till he wrinkled and his hair turned dry as straw and still smell it on him.

A local deputy approached. He leaned on Durward's cruiser to pull off booties sodden with blood.

"I know the Mathers family. Arrested them enough," the deputy said to Danny.

"That them in there?" Danny was crouched now, studying the growing tube of ash between his fingers.

"A few of them. Big clan. I think I can eye-dee Howard

Mathers, Del's younger brother. His Uncle John. His mother, Juanita. And Beth-Ann, his wife. Common law."

"And Del turned into a eunuch out on Eight Mile," Danny said. "Shitty day to be a Mathers."

"The fobbits are taking prints. They'll confirm what I'm telling you." The deputy went to his own vehicle to answer a radio call.

Danny stepped away from the tangle of vehicles spread around the broad turnaround. The strobing light bars under the swaying limbs of a big willow. He stood looking up at the graying sky. He smoked the Marlboro to the filter and stubbed it cold on his boot heel. He put the stub in his shirt pocket. Maintaining site discipline.

Elliott Crabb trotted to him from the swirling lights. He was swinging a pair of oversized evidence bags. He held them up for Danny. Each held a black oilskin raincoat or slicker. Drover's coats. The clear plastic bags were smeared red on the inside.

"They wore these while they worked," Elliott said. "Kept most of the blood off their clothes."

"Those gonna give us any indication of the size of men we're looking for?" Danny said.

"I'm thinking they found these on site. There's three more just like them hanging in the mudroom. Given the boot prints we've found, these must have fit the home invaders like tents."

"Bound to be some prints."

"We also found tie wraps. Cut ones around a kitchen chair set in the great room," Elliott said.

"They made somebody watch all that." Danny crouched again, took a handful of gravel in his fingers.

"Delbert, most likely. Had their fun and then took him out to Eight Mile."

"Shit," Danny said. He dashed the handful of gravel to the ground and stood.

"Where's the squirrely looking dude on your team? The one with the soul patch," he said.

"Derek? What do you need him for?" Elliott said.

"Want to see if I can snake another butt off him," Danny said. He walked back to the slaughterhouse, vivid in the play of carnival lights across its face.

Gunny Leffertz said:
"Keep telling yourself. It could be worse. It could get worse."

30

He lay on a cool, rough surface.

He willed himself to lie still as consciousness returned.

Eyes closed, relaxed in the posture of the insensate, he listened.

Two voices. One commanding. One obliging. Spanish. Mexican gutter slang. Their feet crunched on gravel. The sound echoed off surrounding trees. A night wind whispered through the leaves. The surface he lay on was large aggregate fill, not road quality stone. Someone had moved him to this place.

He lay on his side. He was stripped to the skin. His hands were tie-wrapped before him. His legs were free. There was an uncomfortable pressure in his groin. Source unknown.

A sharp boot toe kicked him in the lower back. He feigned the noises of someone slowly rising back to awareness. He opened his eyes to slits. A skinny guy in a rodeo shirt crouched by him, a cigarette clamped in yellow teeth.

"Welcome back, fucker," the skinny guy said in accented English.

A figure behind Levon guffawed.

"You kill Sabio. Bad idea, fucker. Sabio would have kept you alive a little bit," the skinny guy said.

"The Elvis looking dude in the kitchen?" Levon said.

The skinny guy repeated this to his partner in Spanish. The guffaw rose to a titter.

"I didn't like him. But you should not have kill him. Now we got to do this, fucker."

The skinny stood, gesturing to his amigo who joined him. Together they lifted Levon to his feet. The pressure in his groin turned to a sharp pain. Something was pulling on his genitals, a constricting weight.

They were beside a stretch of train track that ran through deep woods. A Dodge Ram was parked up the track a ways. The motor was running, sending wisps of exhaust into the trees. A steel cable was hooked over the trailer ball under the rear bumper. The cable slack lay in loops from the rear of the truck to where it ended at Levon's feet. The near end of the cable was tightly cinched at the base of his genitals.

"We going to see how fast you run, fucker. *Puedes corer rapido*, fucker?"

The other guy, a chubby guy with a baby face and the gimlet eyes of an idiot, bent double sniggering.

"Turn you from an American to a *maricon, sí*?" Skinny said.

The idiot got it without translation and exploded with a new peal of laughter.

Levon ignored them. He looked to the cable and truck. Fifty feet of cable roughly. The hoop over the trailer ball was run through a ring loop to make a slip knot. He could assume the cinch around the root of his manhood was the same. As the slack was taken up the cinch would tighten.

"Well, we going to say goodbye now. *Trate de mantenerse con nosotros, de acuerdo*? Okay?" The skinny guy clapped him on the shoulder.

"*Vamos*, Memo." The two men left him to march to the truck.

"*Es mi turno*, Beto." The idiot turning to grin back at Levon standing naked on the grading.

"*Sí, hermano. Yo prometi*," the skinny guy said.

Levon watched the men climb into the truck cab. The idiot was driving.

Taking a series of deep breaths, Levon placed one foot before the other, bracing himself on the rough stone. He ignored the pains complaining all over his body. From either the car crash, a beating or both, Levon could feel the effect of deep bruising to his legs, arms and back. His first lungful of air created a lancing pain in his side. A popped rib maybe. Felt more like a stress wound. His eyes were locked on the rear window of the cab. Neither man was looking back at him yet.

A gout of blue smoke from the exhaust pipe and the truck jerked forward spraying gravel. The higher voice of the skinny guy calling for the idiot to take it slow. The truck crawled along the tracks.

They were going to play with Levon.

The skinny guy looked back through the rear window of the cab. Levon faked a limp and an unsteady gait. A flash of those yellow teeth before the face turned away.

Levon broke into a loping run, staying aware not to trip over one of the loops of cable now sliding over the ground as the truck dragged it forward. He could not fall. To fall was to lose.

Without the use of his hands he lost some of his ability to balance. He dropped his shoulders to lower his center of gravity. He ran in a side to side motion closer to a long distance skater, his shoulders moving forward and back to provide more stability.

The loops were closing as the length of cable worked out the kinks to straighten out behind the truck.

He picked up speed. Legs pumping. The sharp stones gashed the soles of his feet. Blood ran free down his legs as the coarse steel cinch sawed against the tender skin of his groin.

The idiot turned his head to look back at Levon. His eyes grew wide. The skinny guy turned as well.

Levon drove himself harder. The skinny guy shrieked commands.

"*Detener! Detener el camion*, Memo!"

Instead, Memo punched the accelerator and the truck leapt forward, back wheels spinning in the loose ballast. The tires caught and the Ram tore off with a roar. The cable was sliding up behind Levon as he ran, catching up to him. Once the last coil passed him the line would go taut.

Levon raced to close the gap. Flying gravel pelted his thighs and shins. He launched himself forward in a spring.

The tie wrap between his wrists caught over the trailer ball. The force wrenched Levon's arms. His shoulders burned with a new blaze of pain. The truck was dragging him now, gravel digging into the flesh of his legs. The terrible pressure on his groin was alleviated. He gripped the ball with numbing hands, his fingers searching the mount for the pin that held the ball in place.

His fingers touched the steel hoop of a cotter pin on one side of the mount and a pair of flanged wires on the other. Over the engine and road sounds he could hear the arguing voices from the cab.

He pressed and pulled on the rusted steel of the cotter pin and pulled it free. The heavy trailer hitch came free, the steel barrel sliding from the box mount.

Gunny Leffertz said:
"You just gonna lie there and die on me?"

31

The truck slowed to a sudden, juddering halt. Levon tumbled free, the thirty-pound trailer hitch hugged against him as he slid over the grading away from the tracks. The long loops of steel cable rattled and sang along with him. He moved as fast as he could manage, making sure to keep his feet clear of the contracting hoops. A single tangle and he'd go down hard.

He was into the weeds along the tracks and heading for a tree line of birches and sumac. The doors of the Ram creaked and slammed behind him. He pelted over a packed gravel service road that ran alongside the tracks.

"*El esta aqui! Ahi!*" Skinny's voice echoed in the clearing.

Levon was into the gloom of the woods as the first rounds wicketed past over his head. He stopped fifty yards into the shadows and took cover behind a tree bole.

A flurry of gun fire from the tracks. Red tracers flashed away to his left in shallow arcs. The shots died away, replaced by a shouted exchange between the men by the truck. The engine noise died. They'd take the keys with them. That escape route was eliminated.

As quickly as he could Levon gathered the long length of steel wire to him, rolling it into loops. He placed his arm through the loops to hang them over his shoulder. The trailer hitch held under one arm, he explored the cinch above his testicles with the tips of his fingers. The wire was slick with his own blood, too slippery for a firm grip.

If he tried to work it loose he risked damaging himself further.

The cable was tight against his crotch around a place holding a major blood vessel. Tear that and he'd die here, bleeding out until he lost consciousness.

The voices were closer but off to the left. Boots tromped in the brush. The two men cursed. First at one another and then at Levon, invisible to them in the black between the trees. Skinny called out dire threats, straining his imagination to find a fate worse than the one their prisoner just escaped.

Levon crouched low, back to the tree, the trailer hitch hugged to him. He listened to the men wander past him and off to the right in the woods along the track. They were searching back in the direction behind the truck. He waited until they were a good distance away before moving away on the opposite bearing. Moving steady and quiet, he put more space between them.

His head swam. Blood loss and dehydration. The night was warm though cooler in the woods. He trudged on, careful to make as little noise as possible.

After he judged he was three hundred yards along, he turned course to return to the tracks. He stepped from the cover of the woods. The truck was a tiny smudge against the field of gravel glowing pearl-like in the moonlight. He scanned the tracks in either direction before hobbling farther away from the truck, losing sight of it around a wide curve in the rails.

A few hundred yards farther on and he had not come to a crossing or bridge. No road intersected the tracks along this run. He did spy a wooden box set on posts on the verge along the grading. He trotted to it at best speed. It was a CSX utility box placed there for use by rail workers.

Using the ball of the trailer hitch he hammered away at the brass padlock holding the door closed. With a two handed grip on the hitch barrel he swung the weight, denting the hasp and scoring the finish off the lock. He wound up using the ball as a ram to break the dry wood away from the hasp until he had a finger hold to pry the door away.

Levon found what he was looking for inside. A massive bolt cutter with a pair of blades hooked like a bird's beak. There were other tools like pry bars and mallets. And several pairs of heavy leather work gloves. He slid a pair of those on his aching hands.

A long, plaintive bray sounded from the woods back the way he'd come. He turned to see a yellow glow like an artificial sunrise coming through the trees beyond the curve.

He squatted in an awkward pose to place the blades of the cutter on the cable dangling between his legs. Back hunched, he pressed the handles closed. His hands slipped on the rubber handles.

The light around the curve grew brighter. A single source of brilliance came into view, a glowing eye set high above the tracks. A train was coming. The horn sounded again to fill the night with a wavering one-note blare.

With greater urgency, he pressed the handles together. The beak of the cutters slid at an angle, catching in the wound strands of wire rather than severing them. He pulled the handles wide, freeing the blades and setting them again on another part of the wire.

Levon turned his head to see the train approaching. His vision filled with the spotlight glare and the horn blowing hard enough to be felt in his chest. The light and sound were like a physical thing, pounding him under a high tide of sensations.

He went to work again on the cutters. He could feel the strength leaving his arms. His skin had gone dry and hot. He was dehydrating. His body was using the last of the moisture in its reserves.

The train screamed past him, ten feet away. The aurora of light moved on by to light the night beyond. He looked down the length of the train to see box and tubular shapes stretched far back beyond the curve. A long freight moving at top speed, the rock of wheel carriages and squeal of steel on steel more deafening than the noise of the horn.

Back along the dark serpent of freight was a new source of light. A pair of lights moving alongside the train at a slower pace. The lights jiggled up and down, wavering back and forth in the shadow of the tall cars.

The Dodge Ram.

It roared forward until the headlights washed over Levon, white and naked against the black night. He could hear the growl of the truck's engine even over the clank and rumble of the train passing.

With a final press he slammed the handles of the cutter together. The cable dangling beneath his crotch parted with a snapping sound.

Freed from his burden, Levon slid the loops of wire from his shoulder. The truck was nearing, wheels banging on springs, lights swinging crazily.

Levon played out six feet of wire in his gloved hands and swung it over his head. The thirty pounds of trailer hitch was flung out in a wide arc, once, twice before he let it fly.

The ball crashed into the windshield of the Dodge with the combined force of its own weight and the truck's forward momentum. The glass imploded as the trailer ball crashed into the cab.

The truck fishtailed, the rear swinging out until a fender caught on the journal box of a speeding freight car. The Dodge was spun three revolutions, bumper-to-bumper, over the gravel in a shower of sparks and flying steel.

Levon had leapt behind the cover of the utility box. It burst into a blizzard of splinters as the spinning front of the truck struck it. The Ram bounced to a stop farther along the grade minus a door and a tire scraped down to the bare rim.

A ten pound mallet lay in the wreckage of the utility box. Levon picked it up and loped to the Dodge sitting quiet in the wake of the train. The last car of the mile-long freight combo boomed away toward the far hills dark against the stars.

Levon met the skinny guy as he crawled from the cab, face smeared with blood from a ruined nose. The guy looked up at him, yellow teeth visible through torn lips. Levon brained him with two swift blows from the mallet.

There was a silver plated Star pistol in the skinny guy's waistband. Levon picked it up and circled around to where the idiot sat dazed on the passenger side. The man was bleeding from where his ear dangled by a ribbon of flesh. One eye was already swelling closed above a deep gash in his cheek.

Levon pressed the barrel of the Star against the idiot's temple and spoke to him in fluent Spanish.

"Put your hands on the dashboard," Levon said.

The idiot obeyed, fingers clutching the curved dash top sprinkled with beads of safety glass.

"I'm going to step back and you're going to step from the car."

The idiot nodded and did as he was told, moving with a deliberate sloth-like pace. His sad eyes were locked on Levon's face. Levon ordered the idiot to, thumb and index finger only, remove the revolver tucked under his belt. The man-child did so. Levon gestured for him to step clear of the cab with his hands held away from him.

"Are you going to kill me?" the idiot said. His voice was a pathetic mewl. A child begging to avoid punishment for some minor infraction.

"I'm not going to kill you," Levon said in fluent Spanish.

The idiot beamed a broad smile showing the jagged edges of teeth broken in the crash.

"Not until you're done changing the tire," Levon said.

In English this time.

32

He made it back to Uncle Fern's. He could not remember the drive.

Fern found him lying passed out by the battered Dodge.

His next memory was waking up in his own bed, sunlight peeping around the drawn shades. He was hooked to an IV bag that read FOR VETERINARY USE ONLY.

"Shit," he said to himself.

He dropped back into a deep stupor.

It was evening when he opened his eyes. He was still heavily sedated and the world looked pink around the edges. Merry sat by the bed on a kitchen chair, reading a book by the light of a lamp on the bedside table.

"Honey," he said. His voice was an arid croak.

Merry looked up, fear on her face. She leapt from the chair to call toward the door.

"Jessie! Uncle Fern!"

Levon tried to sit up. His head spun. There were clean white bandages around both of his hands. There were browning blots of blood on the sheets. His feet were bandaged as well in swathes of gauze. His legs were painted in the deep yellow of a disinfectant. Wrapped around his hips was a dressing that looked like an adult diaper. His groin was where he hurt the most even through the meds.

Jessie came into the room followed by Uncle Fern.

"You need to lie back. You've lost a lot of blood," Jessie said. She took his shoulders in her hands and pressed him back. He felt boneless, unable to resist. He let her guide him back onto the pillows.

"What'd you put in me? Dog blood?" he said. It took effort to talk.

"*Now* you're a comedian. Must be the drugs." She smiled. It was a fragile smile. Lines of worry around her eyes and mouth. Merry stood close staring in mute terror.

"I'll be all right, honey. Don't worry," Levon said. He reached out to stroke Merry's arm.

"He will be, Merry. He's out of the woods. Your daddy just needs rest and fluids," Jessie said. She changed the IV bag for another of clear fluid.

Merry nodded, eyes on her father. Her chin pruned with the effort to hold back tears. Uncle Fern took her by the hand and led her from the room. Once the door was closed Levon could hear his uncle's comforting words over Merry's sobbing.

Jessie put the probe of a digital thermometer in Levon's mouth. It beeped. She set it aside to slip a blood pressure cuff over his arm.

"Fern called you?" he said.

"I was already here. He called me when Dale showed up. The burn was going to kill him and I wasn't up to treating it. I called the EMTs. He's at the county hospital in Teeter."

"What did you tell them?"

"Fern handled it. Lied up a storm about Dale getting drunk and passing out too close to a campfire. You Cades are world class at that. Lying."

"I told you to stay in place, Jessie."

"Did you now? Well excuse me for saving your life. And when did I ever do what you told me to?"

"You didn't call an ambulance for me?"

"Your wounds were interesting but treatable," she said. Removing the cuff.

"I . . ." he began. He glanced at the bandage about his hips.

"Well, I'm usually performing that particular operation in reverse. But you'll heal once the stitches are out."

"I'm sorry. I would never have called you."

"We both know it's nothing I haven't seen before." She smiled. Her hand was on his chest.

He closed his eyes, his mouth pressed shut.

"I do believe you'd be blushing right now if you had enough blood in you." Her tinkling laughter filled the room.

He took her hand in his.

"Tell Fern we're safe. There's nobody going to be bothering us now," he said. His eyes were locked on hers. Her smile faded.

"I'm not going to ask what any of that means. But I am going to insist you lay still and let the antibiotics and your own body do the rest." She broke his hold to stand up and inject a dose of something into a port on the IV line. "And, no, this is not doggy drugs. And you got real human blood and plasma. And a tetanus booster. A surgeon at the hospital owed me some favors. He has a prize Paso Fino I saved from foundering last year."

"Now I owe you," Levon said.

"And I plan on collecting," Jessie said. She leaned over the bed and kissed his forehead.

"I'll send Merry back in, all right?" she said at the door.

"Yeah. Send her in."

Merry rushed past Jessie to the bed. Jessie stepped outside, closing the door halfway behind her.

"Do you want some broth? Uncle Fern's making you some," Merry said.

"In a little bit, honey." He stoked her hair.

"Maybe I can read to you? I could start at the beginning. I don't mind." She picked up the book from the bedside table. On the cover a young boy in knight's armor stood at bay against a monstrous two-headed wolf.

"I'd like nothing better in the whole world, honey," he said.

Levon lay back to listen to his little girl read to him of a hero on an endless quest.

33

Danny Huff borrowed a work station at the county building to read the medical examiner's report on the murders at the Mathers house.

He hated visiting autopsy rooms. He'd rather read the results written in cold prose. In his experience, most MEs hated running through a post mortem in person anyway. They got in enough talking when called to court to testify.

Once the torsos found hanging in the Mathers' home had been rejoined with their attendant parts they were positively identified as Juanita Gaye Mathers, Delbert Mathers' mother. Beth-Ann Tolliver-Mathers, Del's common-law wife. Jacob Howard Mathers, his younger brother. John Bedford Knox, his uncle on his mother's side.

The report claimed the bodies were dismembered using some kind of chopping tool. A machete had been ruled out. It was something with a shorter, broader blade. The ME suggested a cane knife, a tool used for cutting sugar stalks. In any case, they were looking for a murder weapon that was unusual outside of Haiti or south Florida.

Every limb had been tied off using tourniquets of the kind of plastic tie-wraps readily available at any home improvement store, auto parts place or electrical supply. The victims had been systematically dismembered while alive and conscious. The bright red blood, rich with oxygen and infused with adrenaline, confirmed that. Each limb had been severed by a series of chops from a right handed person of considerable strength. The wounds were messy ones inflicted by a strong but careless hand.

Times of death were approximate and staggered. The victims

died within a two hour timeframe; their separate ordeals spread across that period. They died one by one leaving a shrinking number of witnesses who knew they were next.

Delbert Mathers, the big stick of the Mathers clan, was left for last. Made to run the marathon on Eight Mile.

Danny finished reading the files and attached them to emails back to the state bureau in Montgomery and to agents at the FBI and DEA as requested. He wrote up a summation of his own in the body of the emails. His theory was there was some kind of turf war happening in the northern part of the county between Mexican nationals and either other Mexicans or locals over the meth trade. Whether they were at the beginning, middle or end of that war he could not confirm. He sent suggestions, bound to fall on deaf ears, to the various agencies suggesting they probe deeper into the Mathers and their associates. He also asked for any word on the jungle telegraph about any Zetas cartel action that might be going on. All the Mexican bodies so far were marked with Zetas tats.

Emails sent. Report completed. Danny stood up, stretched his back, and thought about sipping a couple of ice cold longnecks and staring at some titties for a few hours. Simple pleasures were best, he thought.

His plans for the evening came apart with the appearance of Trooper Durward.

"You don't have good news, do you?" Danny said with a sigh.

Trooper Durward shook his head in his own mournful way.

"There's weird and then there's fucking weird," Danny said after a long walk down the CSX tracks with the trooper.

He played a flashlight over a shattered utility box leaning crooked on its posts. A mile behind him waited a convoy of state and county vehicles and personnel watching for his signal to come do their jobs.

"We got an obvious vehicular accident here but no vehicle other than some chrome, plastic trim, a blown wheel and glass everywhere." Danny crouched to put his spotlight on a coil of steel cable. The end of it gleamed silver from a fresh cut.

"And two deceased muchachos. Both generally fucked up. One with two bullet wounds to the back of the head. The other with his *cabeza* bashed in with what looks like a hammer." Danny stood and walked away from the tracks to the trees. He held an ultraviolet hand lamp out before him. Spots on the gravel showed phosphorescent on the trail leading from the tree line to the previous location of the vanished vehicle.

"And blood all over the place." Danny turned to Trooper Durward. "Does any of it speak to you, Ralph?"

"First impression, sir. These two set up someone else for a run with a noose around their ball sack. Then things went bad for them. Got all turned around somehow."

"That would be my impression too, trooper. And the victim took whatever vehicle they had him chasing after and escaped."

"Do I call in the teams?" Durward said.

"Sure. I want Cheech and Chong identified. Prints. DNA samples. Tire impressions. Paint analysis off the debris. The whole deal."

Durward turned his head to the mike clipped on his shoulder and welcomed the bunny suits down toward the scene.

"And let's contact CSX. See if one of their trains came through during the time window. Maybe one of the crew saw something. Or remember hitting something." Danny snapped off his light and looked up at the stars.

"Put out a BOLO, sir?"

"Excellent suggestion, Ralph. 'Be on the lookout for a balls naked individual driving a severely damaged vehicle of unknown make and model sporting a brand new wheel recently changed. Person of interest will be identifiable by a steel leash tied around his special purpose.' Or words to that effect," Danny said. He regarded Trooper Durward with a weary grin.

34

"Thought you were taking me home," Dale said. He sat with his back to the door of the International Harvester, his bandaged leg propped up on the bench seat.

"This *is* home for a little bit," Fern said. He swung the wheel of the truck up the drive to where his house sat in the green shade.

"There's stuff I'll need," Dale said.

"I went over to your place and packed plenty. You're mostly gonna be healing anyway." Fern brought the truck to a stop. The engine rattled, taking its own time to come to rest.

"You went over to my place?"

"Cleaned up some like Levon told me."

Dale sat a moment listening to the tap and patter of the roughly idling truck. His head was still light with painkillers. The drugs took the edge off the agony in his leg but he could still feel a tingling searing sensation in his foot and ankle. A nurse in the burn unit told him he'd have some trouble there until more of the nerve endings gave up the fight. He could look forward to a numbness in that area once he was healed. His flesh would feel dead and alien to him. Three days and nights in the hospital left him weak. He craved a cigarette more than anything in the whole world and Fern wouldn't let him smoke in the truck.

"My mom?" he said.

"Took care of her too. Buried her behind the kitchen. The clearing filled with milkweed? Buried the other fella too. Way deep in the woods where even I forget where," Fern said.

Dale went to speak. Fern coughed and opened his door.

"Best you not ask any more, nephew," Fern said. He stepped from the truck to pull a sack of Dale's belongings from the truck bed.

Dale struggled out of the cab on his own with the help of a crutch they gave him at the hospital. He was greeted by Levon coming down off the porch, a hitch in his half-brother's step as well.

"You look like shit," Dale said. He leaned against the hood of the still ticking truck to poke a Pall Mall from a pack.

"You look like more of it," Levon said.

"Guess you and me need to talk," Dale said. This was their first meeting since the night Levon found him in the barn.

They limped together over to the carport where Dale sat hip-shot on the hood of the Mustang, his good heel propped on the bumper. Levon stood in the shadows, leaning against the open door frame.

"You need to tell me what you got us into," Levon said.

"What can I say? We stirred a hornet's nest and both of us got stung." Dale blew a stream of smoke from his nostrils.

"Bullshit."

"I didn't mean for any of that to happen like that."

"Bullshit."

"That's all you're gonna say? Bullshit?"

"You didn't take me up that road for any other reason than to see that compound," Levon said.

He stood with hands braced on the roof of the car. His head was lowered, shadowed. Dale could not see his face. Didn't want to see it. Didn't want to have to look into those eyes and lie.

"I had a problem. I was looking for advice." Dale shrugged and flicked ash.

"You were looking for a recruit. You wanted to know if I'd come in with you."

Levon's voice was calm. Just above a whisper. Dale knew the tone and a thrill of icy fear cut through his oxycodone haze.

"Don't lie. Stop lying," Levon said.

"Yeah. I thought maybe you'd be into it." Dale tried for a light tone. It failed with a quaver.

"Into what? Robbing those guys? Is this what you do now? Making like you're still with the county? Is this how you could buy that shotgun?"

"I just look after things. Keep my eyes open."

"For who?"

"The Mathers. Del Mathers and them." Dale took a last drag and fired the filter out into the yard with a flick of his fingers.

"The ones who used to run white up to the shot houses in St. Louis? The ones our daddy drove for sometimes?" Levon looked up then, pushing himself upright off the car.

"It was Reese Mathers back then. Del's daddy."

"What do the Mathers care about some illegals running a meth lab? Have the Mathers moved on to another business?"

"Yeah. They're diversified these days. Crank. Fentanyl. Got growhouses over in Teeter and Yardley."

"And what were they paying you for exactly?" Levon said.

"Like I said. Keeping my eyes open. Reporting back to them," Dale said. He stepped into the sunlight, gait awkward on the loose scree.

"Only you stepped in it and pulled me in after," Levon said. He hobbled after his half-brother, catching up to put Dale's arm in a painful grip.

"I don't know what to do, Goose. I'm sorry. I don't know what to do now." Tears brimmed in Dale's eyes.

"You're gonna leave it to me from here on," Levon said.

Dale nodded, mouth turned down.

"I'll need names and places. Everything you know about the Zetas and the Mathers," Levon said. He gripped Dale's shoulder, pressing hard.

Dale winced and nodded with more vigor.

"Right now we're going in the house. Merry baked a cake for you and you're gonna stop acting like a pussy, put a big old grin on that stupid face and eat a slice as big as your goddamned head."

Levon released Dale's shoulder with a shove. Together they walked to the house; walking wounded come home to heal.

35

Tio Fausto hated baseball.

He also hated sitting in the bright afternoon sun. It was making him sweat like a horse. His camp shirt was sodden through. And he hated the way the wooden bleacher seat was frying his ass. And he hated how the glint of sunlight off of every surface was pushing a migraine deep into his skull despite the almost black wraparounds he wore.

But he decided that it was baseball he hated most of all. If this were a soccer game he would not mind any of these other things. He would be on his feet cheering and punching his fists in the air. It was the crushing tedium of this boring *gabacho* game causing him the most misery.

He was certain he shared this sentiment with most of the crowd. Yet the three stands of bleachers behind home plate were packed in this stadium the *jefe* built for the local team. The people of Agujereada came to these games so as not to displease the *jefe*. They also came for all the cold sodas and beer they could drink. Kids with ice chests handed out chilled bottles and cans to all who wanted them.

There was also music before and after the game. And it was always a popular band from the TV or radio. Today it was Los Hombres Infernal playing lively *corridos* about bandits and revolutionaries and lost love. They played their most popular song before the game: "El Hombre con Nueves Vidas". The man with nine lives. It was a song about the *jefe*. They would certainly play again after the game was over.

And who could complain about the punishing heat? Was not the *jefe* here himself, sitting like any other peon on a skillet-hot bleacher seat with nothing but a folded newspaper for a fan? Was he not sweating into his underwear like all the rest?

The *jefe* was alone among the onlookers in his intense interest in the game. Two of his sons were playing in this junior league match. They were sixteen and fourteen, very athletic young men, standing at first base and right field. They played for the Agujereada Tigres in uniforms of brilliant white with yellow trim and caps. The boys grew up with a passion for baseball that their father indulged.

And if they liked hockey, Fausto thought, their papa would have built them a *pinche* ice rink.

The Tigres opponents were from La Osca, fifty miles west. They were the Diablos and wore white and, of course, red.

The Diablos' sponsor was a Dutch company with a tire plant in La Osca. The gringos in Amsterdam paid for the junior baseball as a gesture of goodwill. It was money well spent to keep the peons happy in their toxic factory doing dangerous work. Though not too much money. The Diablo's stadium was not near as fine as the one the *jefe* built for the Tigres. And the La Osca team wore uniforms passed down from the teams that played in the years before, with patches on the knees and brown perspiration stained permanently on their blouses.

The *jefe* clapped his hands and whooped at some event on the field, its significance lost to *Tio* Fausto. The crowd, as ignorant as Fausto, as to what was happening before them, followed the *jefe's* applause with a thunderous ovation and barked coyote cries. To Fausto it was just boys raising dust on the field to no purpose other than to make him feel old and tired.

And he did feel old and tired today. There was a burden upon him and the weight came from up north.

His brother Sabio was missing. His nephews were both dead. The police report that found its way to him had them listed as homicides. This brought the death tally to an even thirteen men after the massacre of some of his cousins by persons unknown.

Sabio had been sent north to find out who was responsible, who dared war against the *plaza*, against his family. Sabio was most certainly dead now in an unmarked grave or chopped to pieces in a landfill. It did not bear thinking about.

Other police reports informed *Tio* Fausto of other homicides in the same place as his nephews were murdered. At least they made an accounting of themselves before falling though Fausto wished it was more than five dead *gabachos*. And it *would* be more than five, much more, after he spoke to the *jefe* this afternoon.

The game ended in a three point loss for the Tigres. 15-12. The home team slouched back to their dugout, raising a red cloud as they kicked their cleats in the dust the whole way.

Fausto knew better than to try and speak to the *jefe*. The man's face was red in the shade of his broad-brimmed straw fedora. The *jefe* walked away between the bleachers without a word to anyone. The crowd sensed the mood of their patron and exited the stadium as though from a church. Los Hombres packed up their instruments and left swiftly. It was a dark day in Agujereada.

The *jefe* had an air-conditioned trailer set in the shade of some jacarandas outside of the public ballpark he paid for as a gift to the people of his town. Fausto waited in the heat until summoned within by a pair of young Indios. They were the *jefe's* personal bodyguards, twins armed with gold engraved AK-47s and bandoliers of ammo worn old school *bandido* style.

The refrigerated air in the trailer sent a chill over Fausto's forearms and across the back of his neck. The greasy sweat on his back turned to ice water. The touch of his suddenly frigid camp shirt was almost painful.

The trailer was partly an office and partly an entertainment center. Fausto took a seat on the corner of a crushed velvet conversation pit and pretended interest in a game show playing muted on a seventy-inch screen.

His eyes were on an excited contestant bouncing up and down, boobies moving like maracas under a flimsy blouse, while the show's grinning host leered and stabbed at her mouth with a microphone in a way meant to appear obscene.

But *Tio* Fausto's ears were focused on the conversation from the office at the rear of the trailer.

The *jefe* was speaking to his two sons.

"You did not fail. You played like heroes. You played well and with skill," the *jefe* said. His voice was even like a stream moving over rough stones. "This game was *stolen* from you. You were cheated. Those *pendejos* from La Osca are devils in more ways than one."

The *jefe's* voice rose in volume while it deepened in timbre.

"This is not the baseball way! This is not honorable! To flout the rules in the way they did is to bring disgrace to the game! You know this! I know this!"

"*Sí, papa, sí,*" the boys murmured in reply.

"We will meet them again in one month's time. And there will be no cheating at that game, I promise you on the grave of your mother. You will win by many points. Your skill will carry you to victory on that day as it should have done today."

"*Sí, papa, sí.*"

"Do not blame yourselves, boys. Rather, you should blame me. This was my failing. I should have caught their deceit and stopped the game. I will not fail you again."

The rest of the words were muffled so Fausto could not hear. He turned his eyes from the screen to see the *jefe* standing before a carved mahogany desk, hugging his boys to him and speaking so only they could hear his words.

A bar of blinding sunlight filled the trailer as the boys rushed out to rejoin their friends. Fausto stood as the *jefe* beckoned him into the office. Fausto took a chair he was offered and settled into the steer hide cushions. The *jefe* leaned back on his desk and lit a Marlboro with a lighter shaped like a fist-sized human skull.

Fausto began with assurances that the regular payments from the *plaza* in Alabama would see no interruption even if Fausto had to make up for any shortfall from his own pocket. He then laid out the troubles his *plaza* was enduring from these hillbilly *cabrones*. He closed by asking for the *jefe's* guidance and counsel.

The *jefe* gave his advice to Fausto on what to do next and gave his permission for those same actions. The advice was good though the solutions his boss offered would prove expensive in both cash and lives. But what was money, thought *Tio* Fausto. There was so much more to be made across the border. And what were lives so long as they were *Americano* lives?

Fausto departed with many colorful expressions of his gratitude. The *jefe* waved them away with a tolerant smile. He walked to his car, gleaming like a beetle under the blazing yellow sky, awash in a fresh film of sweat. He did not notice the heat any longer. There was work to be done.

Three days later the newspaper in La Osca contained an article on page four lamenting the death of Javier Morales, the beloved coach of the local junior baseball team. Morales was found alongside the Becerros road.

He had been burned alive.

Chained to a tire hung about his neck.

36

The sign for the Almost Heaven Motor Lodge had faded since its glory days to pale pink and salmon. The multi-colored bulbs that once beckoned weary travelers and horny drunks in off of Trouble Creek Pike had been smashed years before by local kids. The sign was also punched through with buckshot and holed from rifles fired by visitors to the county during hunting seasons past.

The L-shaped building wasn't in any better condition. The roof was green with mold. The office and twelve motel rooms sagged on its foundation. Windows were covered in plywood turned gray over the years. The asphalt lot was crumbled from years of weeds pushing up through its surface.

All but one of the doors to the guest rooms were nailed shut. The remaining door was secured in place with heavy steel hinges. A heavy brass barrel lock hung from a shiny hasp screwed in place on the jamb. The plywood screwed down over the window was newer than the stuff covering the other rooms.

Levon Cade stood under the shelter of the fiberglass awning that ran across the long length of the 'L.' The night was quiet but for a rising and falling tide of cicadas chirruping in the woods either side of the road. He listened to the surrounding dark. No sound or lights from the roadway. The motel sat alone on a long stretch of Trouble Creek. In the hours before dawn there was no traffic on the road.

He worked a pry bar around the plywood sheet covering the window of the locked room. The screws came out of the frame with a squeak. He tossed the sheet to the cracked sidewalk. A single pane of dusty glass covered the window below a strip of frosted louvers for ventilation. Levon tore strips of duct tape from a roll and made a crisscross pattern on the glass before punching it in with the hooked end of the pry bar. He swept the jagged edges away from the frame to drop into the room in a tangle of tape.

Hands in heavy gloves, he leaned into the frame to inspect the room inside. The moonlight revealed steel drums, plastic gallon jugs and stacked cases where a bedroom suite should have been. This was a storehouse for the Mathers clan just as Dale described. In the containers were the chemicals needed to cook meth in significant amounts. Lamp oil, hydrochloric acid, ammonia, lye, paint thinner and more.

Pseudoephedrine was the key ingredient in the recipe and getting harder and harder to come by. He couldn't expect to find it here. That precious commodity would be kept in an even more secure location closer to the labs dotted around the county. It was worth more than its weight in gold.

Back in the day a hidden store room like this would be stacked with sugar sacks for the stills. The worse danger to it was ants. Now, each storage site connected to the crank trade was a potential superfund toxic waste site waiting to happen.

He leaned in farther to confirm his decision to enter through the window rather than the door. A heavy chest of drawers left over from Almost Heaven's days as a hot sheet joint sat just inside the doorway. It was turned athwart the entrance. A twelve gauge double barrel was secured to the top of the dresser with the use of a pair of hose clamps screwed down tight into the wood. The shotgun was upside down on the dresser top, its twin barrels aimed squarely at the door. A thin piece of wire ran from the triggers to the doorknob leaving only a shallow loop of slack.

His boots crunched glass into the matted carpet as he stepped inside. He removed the hoop of wire from the doorframe before shoving the dresser aside. The stacked cases contained two-liter cans of toluene, highly flammable paint remover. He took two cans from a case and stacked them by the window. With the blade of a clasp knife he broke the seals on the caps of all the drums. Thick, greasy fumes of lamp oil rose up in the stifling hot air to fill the room.

Levon lifted the pair of paint thinner cans and stepped back through the window. He punched holes in one of them with the blade and tossed it back into the room. The thin liquid glugged from the punctures to pool on the carpet. He stepped back onto the lot. He could see the air swirling where the vapor building up inside was escaping around the top of the sill. The little room was filled to capacity with the fumes from the barrels.

He unscrewed the top of the remaining can and dipped a long length of twisted t-shirt cloth down into the spout until it was sodden with thinner. Levon wiped his hands dry on the legs of the dark mechanics overalls he wore. With the flame of a Bic lighter he lit the end of the cotton rag before flinging it underhand through the window.

A ball of blue flame whooshed through the window with a blast of scalding air that melted the fiberglass awning. Levon was already away across the lot and heading for the road. By the time he was into the woods the first of the barrels inside the motel exploded with a clang and a boom. The leaves all around turned to gleaming gold for a second with the glow of the sudden inferno.

As he climbed the hill through the woods he could hear muffled thunder as each barrel went up, building the blaze to a furnace heat. The roadway below was filled like a bowl with a brimming cloud of black smoke. Within the cloud was the incandescent heart of the fire as Almost Heaven was consumed in a furious maw of chemical heat.

The sky behind him glowed orange from the blaze even as the ridgeline glowed with a ghost light of coming dawn. He topped the ridge to climb down to where he left the Toyota parked at the end of a drive behind a transformer station.

Before getting into the SUV, Levon punched keys on a cell phone he'd picked up the evening before at the Walmart in Haley.

A voice answered after eight rings. An angry voice with the edge of sleep.

"This better be fucking important," the voice said.

"I am calling to tell you we have sent Almost Heaven to Hell tonight. This is but the beginning of your payment for killing our cousins and robbing us," Levon said in perfect Colombian accented Spanish.

The voice at the other end blustered. The only words he probably understood were 'almost' and 'heaven.' But the message was sent.

Levon tossed the cell phone over the fence of the transformer station. He peeled off the heavy canvas gloves, BIC lighter and mechanics overalls, all recent Walmart purchases, and threw them over the fence as well.

He passed no one on the way back to Uncle Fern's as he drove the silent road home through the woods. The only sounds to reach him through the open windows was the rush of dew-damp wind and the distant wail of sirens.

37

"Fuck it," Lou Bragg said to himself.

He rattled two Advils out of the bottle into the palm of his hand. He popped them in his mouth. They washed down with a mouthful of room temperature coffee gone cool during the phone calls coming in all morning.

His head was pounding so hard he couldn't remember if he already took any Advil. Two more wouldn't kill him. He sat at his desk and dared the phone to ring again, dared some dumb son-bitch to call him and add to the pain in his ass as well as his skull.

Lou punched a button on a console by the bank of phones. The vertical blinds covering the southward-facing wall of windows responded, gliding closed with a series of muffled clicks. The blinds shut out the watery early morning light and iron gray sky hanging low over the office towers of downtown St. Louis. He paid a goddamned fortune for a suite on the twentieth floor with a view of the Mississippi. All he wanted now was healing darkness. The bulging ache behind his eyes eased a bit as the room dimmed.

He keyed another button.

"Carlotta, can you take this damn coffee away and bring me in an iced tea?" he said.

"A regular sweet tea?" Carlotta voice said from the speaker box.

He considered that. He glanced at his Rolex. Not even ten o'clock.

"Yes, darling. Regular sweet tea and a boot-load of ice."

"Anything else, Mr. Bragg?" It was "Mr. Bragg" in the office but "Lou" on their regular Wednesday nights over at Carlotta's condo loft in Tower Grove. A condo listed as "additional office space" on the ledgers of Gateway Realty and Title.

"Is my worthless cousin in his office yet?" Lou said.

"In fact, he's right here, Mr. Bragg."

"Tell that son-bitch to stop sniffin' around your desk and get his ass in here." Lou released the key and leaned forward, elbows on the table to rub his fingers into his temples.

His wife said his headaches were just part of a permanent hangover and cautioned him to slow down on the bourbon. His doctor suggested they were a food allergy. Carlotta assured him he just had a big old knot in his head that would come loose with enough tugging. The girl sure worked on that theory on their Wednesday evenings, bless her heart.

Lou Bragg knew it was all the pressure of running Gateway. It all appeared so sweet on paper. Owning an escrow company looked like a perfectly legal scam. The firm had almost a billion dollars in funds on its books. All of it was in separate escrow accounts for pending real estate deals or, by following the laws of the land, profits from deals held in tax-exempt accounts awaiting reinvestment in future land and building contracts. A shifting, morphing heap of ready cash at his disposal and all without the more formal oversights of owning a bank. As long as the books balanced when the escrow's maturation came up on the calendar, no one was the wiser whether money was actually in the fund or perhaps out on the street somewhere earning value.

The perfect slush fund and money laundering vehicle for Lou and his associates' many, less-than-legal interests.

But keeping track of all it was a migraine in waiting. Each account was a ticking clock. Money went in upon settlement or agreement of a real estate sale and it all had to be there on the assigned date at the end of the legal term for such accounts. They were usually six months in duration. That being the legal length of time allowed for money to be held tax-free between investments.

Sometimes it was a race to rake it all back from operations across five states. It was always messy. Loan sharking, guns, gambling, dope, prostitutes, cigarette smuggling, and shot houses were all highly profitable enterprises, to be sure. But they didn't always pay out as steady as they should. Lou and the firm skated damned close to a few shortfalls when commercial real estate developers wanted their funds handy in a hurry to make an unanticipated bid.

He considered, a number of times, making a suggestion to the boys to sell the firm and go back to the old ways of hiding income. Retail stores, restaurants and the casinos had their own complications when it came to washing cash. But, damn it, that had worked for them and their pappies and their pappies before them. Only trying to explain that selling off a golden goose like Gateway Realty and Title because it was giving him killer headaches could cause problems of perception for Lou. The boys might see him as weak. The boys might decide maybe Lou Bragg wasn't as big a man as he'd convinced them he was.

One of the brass-bound double doors swung in followed by Merle Hogue slouching toward the high backed guest chair upholstered in tobacco colored leather. Merle was his mom's sister's oldest and dumbest. The man wore a gray Men's Wearhouse suit too tight by one size. His belly strained against a cheap ass J.C. Penney shirt. His pant legs were speckled with hairs off the pack of hounds he kept in the yard at his redneck mini-mansion out in Olivette.

"Damn, cousin. Spruce yourself up," Lou said.

He tossed Merle a lint roller from inside a desk drawer. Merle went to work running the sticky surface over his pants until the roller was a furry log.

Carlotta arrived with a tall tumbler filled to the top with ice and chilled tea. She swiveled to the desk on high heels, gliding silent over the thick pile carpet. A stripper's body in an Ann Taylor suit. Lou's headache backed off a pace. He wished, by God, it was Wednesday instead of Monday.

"Thank you, darling," Lou said. He took the glass from her manicured fingers and pressed it to his throbbing forehead.

"Is there anything else I can do for you right now, Mr. Bragg?" she said. Her smile was lovely and as fixed on her face as a Texas beauty queen.

"There is not, Carlotta," he said. He watched her walk to the double doors and admired, as he did each time, the pneumatic gift of nature that is woman at her finest.

"There something you needed from me, Lou?" Merle said. "'Cause I needed to run out 'cross the river and look into the matter you and me talked about last week."

Merle talked in ambiguities, practically a second language for him. He insisted on skittering around without ever being specific, or providing details, from his end of any conversation. Merle believed, at any moment, law enforcement agencies—state, local and federal—might be listening in.

Lou had no patience for it this morning. He found Merle's precautions annoying in particular and Merle Hogue annoying in general. Besides, he was paying a security firm a shit ton of cash each month to make certain his office suite was as fortified against all manner of electronic surveillance as the Kremlin.

"Got a call from Roy Mathers down in Haley. I need you to head down there," Lou said.

"What's it about? Not sure I know the guy," Merle said.

"Delbert Mathers' oldest boy down in Alabama. They're having trouble with Mexicans down their way. Got dead Mexicans. Del and some of his family got killed."

"What am I supposed to do about it, Lou?"

"Go down there and do what it takes to straighten things out. The Mathers outfit isn't so big but they earn steady. Always pay up to us with no hiccups. You get your ass to Alabama and make sure it stays that way."

"Mexicans. You mean like a cartel?" Merle said. A bit of color drained from his face.

"Probably cartel. That a problem for you, Merle?"

"Those greasers don't fuck around. I'm as likely to wind up with my throat cut some night."

"Take some of our boys with you then. Granger and Gary Bush maybe. Some of their crew. Tell them I'll cover them on it. Those Mexicans will back off once we put enough of a hurt on them. They're all business, just like us. You need to make it too expensive for them down there."

"I'm gonna be sleeping with one eye open for a while, tell you what," Merle said.

"Today. Get what you need and drive down there. Carlotta'll give you Roy's address. Call me tomorrow with what you find out." Lou sat back in his chair and took a long pull of sweet tea.

Merle knew he'd been dismissed. He rose from the embrace of the guest chair and left the office. The big brass door glided closed, silent on oiled hinges.

Lou Bragg rested his head against the high back of his chair and closed his eyes. Merle could be right. This Mexican business could get ugly. Could get costly. He might just have sent his cousin into an unholy clusterfuck.

Well, he had plenty more cousins.

He sat up and touched the intercom button.

"Carlotta, changed my mind. Bring me a bourbon on ice."

38

They rode with the windows down despite the heat. Brand new windows to replace the ones blown out when the Toyota rolled in the ditch. A brand new door on the driver's side. Cranberry red.

Merry made an airplane of her hand, holding it against the wind rushing by. The clean smell of the woods filled the cab of the Toyota. It had rained that morning. A haze was still rising off the asphalt where the sun reached through the arch of leaves to touch the road surface.

"You're going to be finished fixing your old car soon, right?" Merry said.

It came out of the clear blue. Levon knew that she'd spent the start of the drive playing this conversation out in her mind.

"There's a few things left to do before I get it painted," he said.

"So the barn will be empty," she said.

"Sure. Though Uncle Fern might have plans for his barn seeing as it's his barn."

She went silent a moment. The exchange was not playing as she hoped. A new approach was called for. Something direct to the topic.

"There's room for a horse in there," she said.

He nodded. "Room for three or four."

"Jessie said Bravo's owners are looking to sell. I could pay for him myself. Work it off at the stable."

"A horse is a lot of work."

"Maybe you could get a horse so Bravo's not alone. You like to ride, right?"

"I *can* ride. I don't really *like* to ride. It was part of my job."

"I'll do the work. It's not like it's even work to me. It's fun," she said.

"I know that, honey. But you'll be starting school soon."

"Maybe I could home school."

He turned to see her smiling, eyes dancing.

"Yeah," he said. "My uncle could teach you the proper amount of yeast to put in the mash and I could teach you to field strip a rifle."

"I could do it. I could take care of Bravo all on my own."

"Tell you what. We'll talk to Jessie and see what's what."

"Great." Merry beamed.

He pulled the Toyota to a patch of gravel by the barn and brought it to stop. She jumped from the car. He killed the engine and stepped out, too.

"Are you going to watch me ride?" she said.

"And I'm going to help you get Bravo cross-tied. And I'll be here to help you brush him down," he said.

"You sure you want to?"

"There's no place in the whole world I'd rather be."

They walked to the barn together in a halting gait. She pressed to his side, arms about his waist. He with a hand gripping her shoulder to hold her tight against him.

Gunny Leffertz said:

"You can't see evil by looking for it. Comes in all shapes and sizes. Same as you can't tell how much fight a man has in him just by looking. You're just as likely to have your ass kicked or your throat cut by a little man with a baby face and a child's smile."

39

The man who got off the eight-seater prop was not listed on the passenger manifest.

He was aching from the eight-hour journey up from Old Monterrey in a Piper to a field outside McAllen, Texas and then to a battered Cirrus with sprung seats that landed him rough on an empty highway north of Baton Rouge. A midnight drive to where a Gulfstream waited on a private field. The final leg brought him here to Makepeace Commercial Airfield where he stepped out into the wet air of an Alabama summer.

Two cousins, Carlos and Lupo, met him with the best car they could steal, a two-year-old Audi that now sported Arizona plates. Doctor's plates. They stood by the cyclone fence, waiting for the man in a mix of awe and fear.

El Chistoso.

The Stoneface.

The man approached the gate. Stooped with broad shoulders and the start of a belly over his tooled leather belt. He carried a silk jacket over one arm. No luggage. There was a hitch in his walk. It was the result of a wire bomb from back in the day when the Columbians still thought they could scare the Mexicans back into their place. The same explosion that shattered the man's knee made a landscape of crossed scars over his face and neck. The tiny bits of white-hot wire, hurled his way at ballistic speed, slashed through flesh and nerves leaving him with a face as immobile as a granite carving. It left him with a visage that expressed his true nature. Heartless. Soulless. A man who brought pain to others without a trace of either joy or sympathy.

Carlos held a rear door for him while Lupo raced around to get behind the wheel of the Audi. El Chistoso waved Carlos aside with a grunt and pulled open the front passenger door to take a seat beside Lupo.

The air within the car was chilled. The sweat of Chistoso's Ban-Lon polo shirt turned to ice water. A thrill of cold as he pressed his back to the seat. He let out a long, slow breath while the cousins stared at him as though he were an animal recently escaped from a cage.

"Do you have a phone for me?" Chistoso said. His voice was a grating rumble. More evidence of the damage from the Medellin bomb.

From the back seat, Carlos fumbled in a pocket. He thrust a cell phone forward.

"It is clean, *señor*. We bought it on the way here today."

Chistoso took the phone and thumbed it to life.

"Merle Hogue. He is the one I must speak to. Put in his number." He held the phone back to Carlos who tabbed keys with sweating hands.

"Drive," Chistoso said.

"Where?" Lupo said.

"How am I to know? I have never been to this shithole in my life," Chistoso said. He eyed Lupo from deep within recesses of scar tissue.

The Audi left behind a gush of gravel that tinkled against the chain fence.

40

"You know not to drink when you take those, right?" the girl at the prescription counter said.

"Yeah. I know," Dale said. He was already a six-pack of Miller up on the day and it was only a little past noon.

"Just so you know," she said.

Dale leaned on his aluminum cane and sniffed at her as she finished ringing up his oxy scrip along with a Red Bull and a bag of salt and vinegar chips. Stupid little bitch barely out of high school. Thinks a blue smock turned her into a doctor or something. If she's so damn smart why doesn't she take care of that bumper crop of zits sprouting on her forehead? He snorted but said nothing.

"Be healthy," she said. A professional smile and a hand held out to offer him his plastic sack.

"Yeah. You too," he said. But in a cutting tone. She ignored him to greet the next person in line, a mom with a sniffling kid in her arms.

Out in the Walgreen's parking lot, Dale sat in the cab of his truck and washed down a pair of oxys with a mouthful of warm Miller. The pain in his leg was a constant but the itching from the skin grafts was worse. A torment. They told him the pain would calm down to a simmer once enough scorched nerve endings gave up the ghost. And the itching would subside as the new flesh knitted together. They told him going to physical therapy would help some. Fuck that, he said.

Some guy, a Jew probably, was on the radio talking about how you could make yourself happy just by deciding to be happy. Dale flipped over to the country station. Some warbling bitch singing about how she didn't need a man. He snapped the radio to silence. They never played good stuff like George Strait or Patty Loveless any more.

A tap on the glass shook him. He snapped out of a deep nod, mildly surprised to find himself still parked outside the drug store.

A face leered at him through the smeared passenger window.

"That you, Roy?" Dale said.

"Roll down the window, you dumb son-bitch," Roy Mathers said. The leer was frozen on his face. His peculiar pearl gray eyes fixed on Dale from a sunburnt face. A raised star of white scar tissue creased his cheek. It was a remnant of a .38 slug that passed through his mouth a few years back taking most of his teeth with it.

Dale fumbled for the button on his door panel. The window rolled down and Roy leaned in to help himself to a Miller out of the sack by Dale's hip.

"What can I do you for, Roy?" Dale said.

"Whyn't you stop by the Legion hall? There's somebody I want you to meet," Roy said. He popped the top off the Miller. He flicked his fingers to spray foam off his fingertips.

"I might just do that sometime."

"You should do it right now. Follow me back. Goddamn! It's warm!" Roy flung the beer back into the cab where it gurgled empty on the floor mat.

"Sure. Sure. Okay."

"Follow me back." The leer that passed for Roy's smile turned to a feral snarl revealing his too-bright new teeth. They shone even whiter with his face burnt red.

"Sure. Sure." Dale ground the key to bring the truck to life. Roy headed for his restored '76 Charger. He waved a lazy hand, beckoning Dale to follow.

"Hey, man. Sorry to hear 'bout your daddy," Dale called after him.

Roy turned back as he pulled the Charger's door open. Eyes dead as slate. Dropped his chin one time, slid behind the wheel and peeled away.

Palms damp on the steering wheel, Dale sat a moment watching Roy wedge the big muscle car into traffic on the county road. A honk, a chirp of tires, a squeal of brakes as he cut off a UPS truck. Roy was gone south and out of sight behind the signage in front of a strip mall.

Dale pulled to the exit and considered, for one giddy second, turning left instead of right and driving like hell for the interstate and from there to Chicago or even Quebec. Instead he made the right to follow Roy Mathers back toward Colby.

No idea who it was that Roy wanted him to meet. But Dale decided already that he wouldn't like the son-bitch.

The interior of the Legion hall was hushed. Cool, dry air stirred from a pair of wall units humming above the Stars and Stripes and Stars and Bars hanging side by side from the long wall opposite the bar. Except for the tang of beer skunk the place could have been a church.

Two old guys sat in mumbled conversation at a table. An even older guy sat humped on a stool playing the poker machine at the end of the bar. A black guy known to everybody only as Simms leaned back behind the bar watching a sports channel on the screen above the shelves of bottles; three black guys and a white girl talking and laughing on a set that looked like the bridge of a space ship. Simms was resting his good leg on a stool. His other leg, the steel and wire contraption Uncle Sam had given him, was braced against the duck boards.

Simms was wishing he could turn the volume up on the TV—he was reading the closed captioning and it wasn't the same. But the old cracker playing poker would start bitching for him to turn it down. And that old cracker marched up the boot of Italy in '44, fighting Nazis every step of the way. Simms figured the old boy earned his silence while he nursed his Bud and poured his monthly check into the flashing machine.

The door out to the parking lot swung open letting in a burst of sunlight like from the heart of a furnace. Two men stepped in, the door closing behind them to restore the gloom. One of them was a guy Simms knew as Dale. Came in with the help of a cane. Couldn't recall his last name. Remembered that he was in Iraq, too.

The guy following was Roy Mathers. Simms knew him all right. Knew that the only uniform Mathers ever wore was one-piece and orange.

"We're heading on back," Mathers said. His hand jinked up, finger pointing to the rear of the long room.

"They're waiting on you," Simms said. He nodded to Dale who nodded back before cutting his eyes away. Sad eyes.

Roy led the way through an arch with Dale behind. To one side was a pair of restrooms. To the other a hallway that ended in a sliding accordion door. Roy shoved it open and held it for Dale to enter.

A couple of tables were set up in the windowless room. The walls were lined with cases of empties. Bud. Miller. Coors. The open space in the middle of the room was lit by hanging lamps drawn low over the table tops. Thursday through Saturday this was a poker room for members only. A stubby little man in a cheap gabardine suit sat smoking at one of the tables. Dale didn't know him but thought he might know who he was.

He damn sure knew the man leaning back, arms crossed, against the wall of empties. He knew he didn't like a thing about the guy. Gary Bush was well over six feet with prison muscle straining the chest and sleeves of a Jack Daniels t-shirt. His arms were covered to the wrists with tats. Most prominent on his ham-sized biceps were a noose on one arm with a Maltese cross in the center of the loop and a screaming skull sporting a Confederate kepi on the other. Gary wore a disapproving sneer as he met Dale's eyes. He glanced down at Dale's cane and made a woofing sound between his lips.

"We have a situation here," Merle Hogue said. The stubby little man glanced up at him from under shadowed brows.

"Uh huh." Dale's mouth was dry as dust.

"I represent people who have an interest down here. You know who I might be talking about?" Merle said.

St. Louis, Dale thought but said nothing.

"Roy tells me you been working for his family a couple years now. Tells me you keep an eye out for him and his. You keep him in the picture concerning his family's competition. Like these Mexicans." Merle smeared out what was left of his Chesterfield and lit another from the pack by his hand.

Dale waited.

"Heard you had your own trouble with these Mexicans. They killed your ma. Nearly killed you. You care to share with us why that might be? Why a bunch of greasers have such a hard-on for a small town hillbilly ex-deputy?"

Gary Bush snuffled.

"Guess they thought I was getting too close," Dale said. He lowered his eyes to the floor.

"Too close? Too fucking close? Try point blank, boy. Try so close you have their cousins' and their nephews' and their bastard bambinos' blood all over your hands."

Dale said nothing.

"Now tell me that's not true. Now just try, try and convince me that those wetback motherfuckers weren't after your ass because you killed a bunch of their crew and stole their money and their product." Merle's voice was mocking, playing for Gary Bush who was eating it up.

Dale's fingers danced on the curved handle of his cane.

"Now we have dead Mexes and dead white folks and nobody's happy. And when it's all said and done, business is affected. The money flow has fallen to a piddly little dribble outta this county and the people I represent are displeased. And the *amigos* are a damn sight displeased. And how do we make this right?"

Dale clutched the cane handle, knuckles white.

"We need your help, son. You tell us what happened. Every scrap. And you tell us who helped you. And we'll go easy on you. Otherwise, we have to give you up to the Mexicans. You understand that there's no other way. You understand that your only choice is between the wholly unthinkable and the slightly preferable."

Dale nodded. He could feel his pulse behind his eyes. His throat was in the grip of a fiery fist.

"Tell us, then. Who'd you rob the Mexes with?"

Dale turned to pivot, drawing the barrel of the cane up into his fist as he moved.

He swung the handle of the cane in a wide arc that took Roy Mathers square in the temple. He'd taken the cane apart after the hospital gave it to him and poured eight ounces of molten lead into the hollow of the handle. It was a half-pound hammer that dropped Roy to the floor with a shout.

Gary Bush had pushed himself off the beer cases to launch at Dale. The cane handle came up as Dale shortened his grip. He stabbed out, spearing Gary in the throat with the heavy handle. The big man stumbled. Eyes goggling. Mouth working like a fish caught up on a bank. He hurled himself back to crash into the cases, toppling a tower of them. The bottles spilled out to turn into a shower of glass on the tiles.

Dale moved for Merle who had shoved himself from the table in a crouch. His teeth had bitten the end from his cigarette. His chubby hands clawed for a revolver in his waistband. Dale raised the cane over his head for a downward blow aimed at the smaller man's skull.

Before he could drop the hammer his elbow was hooked by an arm from behind him. Dale half-turned his head to look into Roy Mather's face. Twisted in blind rage and painted crimson with blood where the cane handle opened his brow.

Roy raised an automatic in his hand. A big nickel-plated job. It came down on the back of Dale's neck. Once. Twice. Then Dale felt nothing. Knew nothing.

41

The day was dying but the heat remained. The air grew thicker as the sky darkened, a cloying stickiness unrelieved in the still air that lay between the hills.

Clouds of moths gathered under the pole lamp on the gravel lot along the farm road. Just as the insects were drawn to the light, dozens of farm workers walked from the rows of cinderblock huts to line up at the food truck parked in the pool of light. They lined up, paid, and retreated either to their temporary homes or to the picnic tables set in the shadows of the pines that loomed around the lot. Children chased each other in and out of the light. The blue glow of tiny screens were visible in the gloom.

El Chistoso watched from the air-conditioned interior of the Audi. This could be his family, his mother and father and brothers, many years ago. But for the firefly glow of the smart phones, this could have been an evening in the camps after a long day of picking tomatoes, string beans or melons. Even the food offered by the truck was the same. Pork. Pulled beef. Chicken. Barbecued corn. Beans and tortillas. Peasant food. All washed down with an orange soda and, if there was enough money, an ice cream. Often he had to share a cone with a brother. Each taking turns to lick the scoop of vanilla or chocolate, fighting over the last bite of the sweet cake cone.

He nudged the dozing boy behind the wheel.

"*Que, jefe?*" Lupo said.

"*Helados,*" Chistoso said and pointed at the truck.

"What flavor?"

"Whatever they have."

Lupo climbed from the car and joined the line at the truck. On the dash, the cell phone buzzed.

Chistoso put it to his ear. A voice he did not know was speaking.

"*Un momento,*" he said. He handed the phone back to Carlos who listened a while. Chistoso turned the rearview mirror to watch Carlos listen.

"It is the man, Merle Hogue, who says they have one of the *yanqui* who took the money. He says the *yanqui* has told them all he knows. There was another who helped him. They will find him for us," Carlos said.

"What of the *yanqui* who told them this?" Chistoso said. His eyes were on Carlos' reflection in the mirror. Carlos repeated the question in English. He met Chistoso's eyes in the glass and shook his head.

"Tell the man I want the other *yanqui* alive. I insist on it," Chistoso said.

"As soon as they find him, *jefe*. They promise. He will be yours," Carlos said after repeating the question and receiving the answer.

Lupo returned with a cone for each of them. They sat in the car eating ice cream. The cold confection chilled Chistoso's tongue but little more. The sweetness of the treat was something he could only experience in memory. Another sensation the Colombians had robbed from him.

Gunny Leffertz said:

"You kill the man or he kills you. Ain't no half-stepping."

42

Dragonflies hummed over the tops of the grass. Drops of dew shone like diamonds in the mid-morning sun.

From within the house came the baying of hounds.

The car crunched to a stop in front of the house. An El Camino. Lovingly restored. Jet black with metal flake finish. Custom wheels and fat tires. A real redneck war machine.

Men got out either side of the cab. White guys. Boots, jeans, madras print shirts pressed to a razor edge. They looked like catalog models pretending to be telephone linemen.

One walked toward Uncle Fern's front porch. The other remained behind to slide a pump shotgun from a sleeve mounted on the seat back. The one walking to the house slid a stainless steel revolver from under his shirt.

The shotgun man turned to scan the landscape too late to see Levon step from the shadows of the barn. Levon was hunched forward, walking fast, his .45 in a two-handed grip.

The shotgun man threw the stock of the Remington to his shoulder. Levon's first shot punched a hole in the Camino's door. The shotgun man flinched left. The second round took him in the chest below his armpit. He spun to slam into the fender. His grip weakened on the shotgun. He watched it fall into a spray of his own blood. The third shot lifted him up on his toes. He didn't feel it. The back of his skull was gone, spinning away into the grass like a pie plate.

The second man ran for the cover of the porch, ducking low. The dogs in the house were going mad. He held the revolver away from him, firing blind shots straight armed. A slug passed him within inches to tear into the shrubs with a brittle snap. He reached the bottom steps of the porch and the cover of the railings when the door of the house exploded open. The big dogs raced for him, howling with fury. All but one. The ridgeback moved in low to get a mouthful of the gunman's thigh just below the crotch.

He stumbled backwards, flailing down the steps, legs tangled with the bodies of the dogs. A terrible pain shot up from where the ridgeback worked its teeth deeper into his flesh, twisting its head for better purchase.

His animal shriek was cut short by a blast of twin thunder.

Fern stood braced in the open screen door. A twelve gauge, both barrels smoking, in his fists.

The gunman lay in the dust. A generous chunk of one shoulder and most of his head turned to gleaming gristle. The hounds, alarmed by the noise and scent of human blood, tore away into the trees, wailing in terror. Only the ridgeback remained, standing over the fallen man. Snout clotted red, tongue lolling in a canine smile.

"Sure hope they weren't just stopping for directions," Fern shouted to be heard over the ringing in his ears.

Levon paused by the headless man to dig though the man's pockets. In one pocket he found a ring of car keys. He came up with a smart phone in another and tabbed it to life. There was a fresh text on the screen from RMATHERS.

any luck

at the brn

u meet us here

He tabbed a reply and sent a message back under the name LONEGRANGER.

nthng here

heading yr way

He wiped the blood from the phone onto his jeans and stuck it in his shirt pocket.

"You're going to have to get the backhoe out again, Fern," Levon said. He stepped away across the gravel to trot into the house.

"Suppose that's best," Fern said.

The smart phone trilled. Levon read the reply.

Suprize 4 u wen u gt here

"We still have family in Murfreesboro?" Levon called as he stepped from the house, Fern's Winchester lever action under his arm. A box of shells in his hand.

"Cousin Wendell and his wife."

"You better go see them a while," Levon said. He tossed the rifle and shells onto the seat of the El Camino.

"Suppose that's best, too," Fern said.

Levon gunned the El Camino to life. A one-eighty spin sprayed dust and stone and he was gone down the driveway in a cloud of blue exhaust.

"Get away from there, feller," Fern said. He waved the ridgeback off the corpse. Flies were already gathering, green backs shimmering.

The dog loped into the cool shadows under the porch to lick its paws clean.

43

Sandy backed out of a stall with a forkful of straw and droppings. She became aware she wasn't alone. A shadow fell across the floor by the wheelbarrow nearly filled with muck. She hadn't heard anyone come in over the music from the radio resting on a shelf outside the tack room.

A man with a sunburnt red face. Creepy pale eyes. Butterfly bandages set in a row on his forehead. Tasha, a buckskin mare, shared Sandy's surprise. She stomped and huffed in her stall at the man's arrival.

"You alone here?" he said.

"My mom's out riding. She'll be back soon," Sandy said.

"*She* alone?" The man reached out to snap the radio off.

"She's with a friend of ours."

"That big guy?" The man tried a smile. It was unnaturally white in his ruddy, peeling face.

"No. Someone else." Sandy tightened her grip on the handle of the fork. Her eyes moved past him. Two more men were out in the sunlight standing by a muscle car.

"He been around?"

"Who?"

"Levon Cade. I heard he comes around here sometimes."

"I haven't seen him. Not in a while," Sandy lied.

"Someone told me he's got the hots for your mom."

Sandy took an involuntary step back.

"She pretty like you? I'll bet she is. Apple don't fall far, does it?" He matched her step, closing the gap between them.

"Maybe you can come back later. She's out for a long ride. Might be the rest of the day." Sandy stepped away again. The handle of the rake rattled against the boards of the stall. She let out a breath when the cell on the man's belt buzzed.

He plucked it off his belt, read the screen and frowned. She thought about trying to get by him, make it to the house. One of the men outside said something and the other laughed. The sunburnt man's brows knitted down over dove gray eyes as he focused on the screen. Rough hands awkward as he keyed a reply. He hooked the phone back on his belt and turned his eyes to Sandy.

"You like to ride? This horse yours?" he said. His thumb jerked at Tasha's stall.

"My horse is out in the field. This one's inside 'cause she's getting ready to foal."

"That so? You ride too. Bet you look pretty when you ride. Nothing prettier than a pretty girl up on a horse," he said. He stepped closer to come to rest, leaning a shoulder against a stall post. Only an arm's length from her.

She fought to keep her hands still on the fork handle. The tines began to hum with the force of her grip.

"I don't want to hurt you, see? I want you to like me. Because I like you. I think we can get along just fine," he said. His voice had dropped to a whisper. A smile quavered at the corners of his lips. His eyes studied her with a cold gaze, a serpent's gaze. She felt as though she was stripped naked.

"I told you. My mom's not here. And Mr. Cade's not here. Maybe you can come back some other time."

The man pushed off the post. His smile went crooked. He reached behind his back. His hand came out with a shiny steel gun in his fist. He aimed it over the stall door and fired point blank at the mare.

The report of the gun filled the barn with thunder. The girl's scream was lost under the high pitched squeal from Tasha. The big animal staggered, then fell hard against the timbers of a stall wall. She dropped down on the ground, her legs gone lifeless beneath her.

Sandy threw the fork aside to launch herself to the mare's stall. Before the man snaked an arm about her neck she caught a glimpse of Tasha lying on the floor. Hooves kicking feebly in the straw. A pathetic bleating coming from her mouth, the big teeth bared and smeared red. Eyes white all around. The hair down her flanks were streaked with blood from a ragged wound torn in her hide.

The sunburnt man drew Sandy closer until only her toes touched the floor. He whispered in her ear. His hot breath was rancid like sweet feed gone bad at the bottom of a bin.

"See? Like I told you. I don't want to hurt you. But I will kill every fucking nag on this place if you keep lying to me." He tightened his grip. She saw white stars shimmering around the edges of her vision.

A voice called from outside. "Roy? Hey, Roy."

"Yeah?" He loosened his hold. Her boot heels were on the ground again. She was still pressed against the heat of him.

"Granger's coming."

"See what he wants," the sunburnt man said. "Tell him I'll be out in a minute or so."

Gunny Leffertz said:
"Never, ever surrender your weapon. Never. Ever."

44

He floored the El Camino across the lot in front of the stable.

Levon centered the car on the nearest gunman. The bumper took the man across the knees. His head bounced once off the hood leaving a bloody dent behind. He then vanished under the front of the car. Levon felt the rear left tire lift as it crushed what life was left in the man.

The Camino came to a juddering sideways stop in a thick cloud of red dust. Levon came around the front at a run as the engine died behind him. The Winchester carbine to his shoulder. A big man wearing a wifebeater was backing to the open stable doors. His arms covered in a dense inked tapestry. He had a big bore revolver up, firing wild. One slug crazed the windshield of the Camino. A second kicked up a cyclone of dust ten feet in front of Levon's boots.

On the run, Levon hit the big man with a heavy slug from the carbine. The man bent double over a .44 magnum round low to the guts. A second shot punched through his chest. A third dropped him, arms splayed, to bang against a door, sending it swinging.

Levon jacked a fresh round into the carbine as he stepped over the big man into the dimness of the stable. A deep cough, a wet sputtering, echoed off the steel roof. In the aisle before him a red-faced man scuttled sideways. He had Sandy pressed against him in a chokehold. A nickel-plated automatic held hard against her side. The girl gasped for air. Her face darkened with the effort. The toes of her wellies tapped an uneven rhythm on the floor.

Levon kept on his steady stride toward them. The carbine to his shoulder. The man's head in the half-moon sight.

"Drop the gun or I'll do her right now." The man's voice was thin, rising to another octave.

"That's not going to work." Levon kept on closing.

"It's the best I'm offering." The guy smiled now. A near phosphorescent grin.

"I meant for you," Levon said.

The round took the man just below the right eye. There was a flower of blood and brains blooming behind him. His arms, inanimate objects now, dropped to release Sandy from his grip. The automatic spun to rest in the dust.

Roy Mathers fell backwards to a seated position, head bobbing, to collapse onto his back. One heel dug a furrow in the dirt until the signals coming from the half a brain he had left died away.

Sandy stood, shoulders hunched. She stared at Levon in mute shock. He kept the carbine shouldered to step between her and the dead man. He put two more rounds in Roy's chest before stepping to the stall door where the mare lay screaming. He leaned over the door to pump two rounds into the animal's head. It went limp instantly. The stable was silent once more but for a mewling sound from the girl.

Levon stepped to her, putting a hand to her cheek and turning her face to his. She flinched but he kept his hand there until their eyes met.

"Where's Jessie and Merry?" he said.

"Up on the high trail. Heading back by now," she said. It was the voice of a child years her junior. Her eyes swam in her head, pupils dancing.

"You and I are going to ride up to meet them. We're taking whatever horses are left with us so they'll be safe."

Her eyes moved to Tasha's stall. He pressed his fingers in her cheek until she looked at him again.

"You go into the house and change your clothes. Grab some food. Canned stuff. A loaf of bread. And some blankets. Then meet me in the field to help bring the horses in."

She nodded, eyes on his.

"Look straight at the house. Don't look anywhere else. You hear me, Sandy?"

She nodded again. More vigorous this time. Her eyes lost some of their glassy look.

"Go on now. That's a good girl," he said.

45

Carlos offered to find them a motel where they could wait in comfort. Chistoso did not respond. He only sat in the car listening to a distant Spanish language station. Band music faded in and out under waves of static. The older man would not allow him to change it.

They were parked behind a RaceTrac watching the sun drop behind the top of the pines. Lupo was in the convenience store getting coffee and treats for them. The old man's sweet tooth was insatiable. Carlos envied Lupo for being allowed to exit the car. He was certain that Lupo was sneaking a cigarette or two out of the old man's sight. Chistoso would not allow them to smoke in the car and would not allow them to leave the car. Carlos was dying for a cigarette or a snort of *coca* or anything to relieve the tedium of hours and hours spent either driving back roads or parked for no reason. His back ached, his ass itched, his eyes felt sandy. The old man sat contented as a sphinx while night turned to day and was turning to night once again.

The old man leaned from his seat to turn the radio off.

"Call the man again," El Chistoso said.

Carlos took the burner from the dash and hit redial.

"Y'ello," the gringo on the other end said.

Carlos glanced at the *viejo* who nodded. Carlos sighed.

"The *jefe* wants to know what is going on," Carlos said.

"Well, it looks like there might be a snag or two on our end," the gringo named Merle Hogue said. He drew the words out. He was hesitant. The news was not good.

Carlos waited. He could hear the man's exhalations. The man was taking long drags on a cigarette.

"I haven't heard from the boys I sent out. I been calling but there's no answer."

Carlos relayed the reply in Spanish. Chistoso blinked.

"The *jefe* is tired of your excuses. Tired of your fuck ups. He thinks it is time we do what you cannot do."

"You think you'll have better luck cleaning up this shitty mess then you and your amigos are welcome to it."

"Tell us the name of the man we want. Tell us where to find him."

"I can tell you where my boy was the last time I spoke to him. You got GPS there?"

"*Sí*. Text the place to this number. We will find it."

"*Mi* clusterfuck *es su* clusterfuck, buddy," Merle Hogue said. He broke the connection.

The burner bleated once. The GPS coordinates were in a new text.

"Get more hombres," El Chistoso said. "Tell them to meet us there."

Carlos swung the Audi around the front of the RaceTrac to find Lupo standing on the walk in front of the store taking a last pull on a Marlboro. He picked up a coffee carrier and plastic sack and trotted to the Audi.

"I fucking hate you," Carlos said in English.

Lupo slid into the rear seat. He handed forward the sack of goodies. The old man dug into it with eager hands. Carlos tossed the burner back to the rear seat. Lupo caught it and looked at the screen.

"I know where this is," Lupo said.

"Good for you. Call the crew. Tell them to get their asses over there and wait for us," Carlos said.

"*Muy bueno*," the old man said. Crumbs of a Little Debbie on his chin.

Gunny Leffertz said:
"If you have to go to ground, go to ground you know."

46

The shadows were lengthening in the tall pines.

They met Jessie and Merry returning down the longer horse trail on the way back to the stable.

Merry wore a smile that broadened when she saw her father riding to meet them. Jessie knew something was wrong. Levon and Sandy were both mounted and Sandy led the Bromley's quarter horse, Juice, and the pony, Montana, on a lead rope. A pack bundle of rolled blankets and knapsacks was tied down on Juice's saddle. Levon had a rifle resting across his pommel. Sandy's face was drained white, reins shaking in her hands.

"What's wrong?" Jessie said.

"They shot Tasha!" Sandy said. Fresh tears started from her eyes. Her mouth was twisted.

"We need to ride back the way you came," Levon said. He drew alongside Merry.

"Not until I know what's going on," Jessie said. Her eyes were hard on Levon's.

"I'll tell you on the way. For now, we all need to keep moving," Levon said. He leaned from the saddle and took Merry's reins. He led her pony around to head back up the trail.

"He means it, Jessie," Merry said.

They left the trail at its northernmost point where it curved back west to rejoin the short trail. The ground sloped up easy and was dotted with tall pines. The ground was clear beneath, the underbrush either shaded out or unable to find purchase in acidic earth composed of decades of rotten needles.

Levon took the lead with Jessie just behind. The young girls were together behind them, Sandy bringing along the pack horse and pony. They rode easy, letting the horses set the pace. A steady pace that made distance was more important than speed. Wear the horses out and they'd be left to go forward on foot.

"We have until sundown to make an easy ten or so miles," Levon said.

"This heads up into the watershed. State land," Jessie said.

"I know. We'll see the posts just ahead. There's a spring where we can water the horses," he said.

"They smell it," she said. Her mount raised his snout, nostrils flared. His lips clamped together with a clopping sound.

They rode through the soundless woods. The bare boles of trees seemed to stretch to infinity in every direction. This was a place to get lost in. And lots of unwary hikers had done so, wandering in ever widening circles until exhaustion or exposure claimed them.

"Tell me why we're not calling the police," Jessie said.

"Because they can't end this. They can't protect us," he said. He kept his voice low so the girls behind them, particularly Sandy, could not hear him.

"And you can end it?" She lowered her voice as well. There was a sharp edge of skepticism in her words.

"I killed three men at your place. Men who were going to hurt your daughter. Do worse than hurt her."

"You could claim self-defense."

"That means getting booked, arraigned and going to county to await trial. They can reach me there. And if they couldn't, they can reach you and Sandy."

"You're trying to scare me."

"I hope I am scaring you, Jessie. Scared is exactly what you need to be right now."

"Okay. I'm scared, okay? So how do you end this?" she said.

"Two ways. Make them think that they got what they're looking for. Or convince them that pursuing me any more is going to be too costly for them," he said.

"Have you decided? Which is it going to be?" Jessie said.

"Both," Levon said.

Steel signs, rusted around the edges, informed them that they were on restricted state land. It cautioned them against trespassing and promised stiff fines for anyone caught camping or lighting fires.

They watered the horses at a spring that bubbled from rocks on the floor of a shallow depression. Cold, clear water from deep within the heart of the long hill they were climbing. Levon topped off some gallon jugs that he handed back to Jessie. Merry stood away from them talking softly to Sandy. The girl looked numb, her eyes on the younger girl speaking low and even, a hand on her arm.

"Your little one is as tough as you," Jessie said. She watched the two girls talking.

"She's a good girl. I don't want her becoming hard. I try to keep her away from things. Not much luck lately," Levon said.

"You're trying. You brought her home."

"This isn't my home any more. It's changed. Something ugly happened."

"Something you're trying to make right? All by yourself?"

"I only wanted to come back to hide. Find some peace maybe. I wasn't looking for this. Now I've dropped you and your girl into this mess with me."

"If that's an apology you can shove it up your ass, Levon."

He glanced up at her, an eyebrow arched. He handed her a full jug to be tied back on the saddle of the pack horse.

"We can walk the horses from here," he said.

"You know where we're going?" she said.

"I do."

They camped cold that night. The horses and pony were hitched to a line strung between trees.

The air turned icy as the moon rose. Jessie held the girls huddled to her under layers of the blankets Levon had packed along.

Levon sat draped in a blanket with his back to a tree. The rifle rested across his knees. He listened to the dark all around. His ears searched through the rising and falling sounds of cicadas for noises that did not belong. A crunch and snap above him turned out to be a line of whitetail deer moving through the pines.

Sandy made a whimpering sound. Jessie pulled her daughter closer, cooing to her in a dozy way until both were silent once more.

The high country of the watershed was far from any road. No highway sounds reached them here. The only sign of civilization was a silver glow against the clouds from the lights in Haley, miles away to the north.

He allowed himself to drop into a state of half-wakefulness. He rested rather than slept. His senses tuned only for sights and sounds alien to this place.

Levon came full awake, not sure what roused him. The pines were gray under a sky lit by the sun still climbing the hill behind them. A white mist hung above the forest bed. Nothing moved. The cicada rhythm had died away leaving a silence that was deep and wide.

Except for a burring sound, waxing and waning, from somewhere far below them. A machine sound. The sound of men.

47

"Get the horses saddled. Leave everything else behind," Levon said once he had Jessie and the girls up and awake.

The high whine of four-stroke engines cut through the morning silence. The noise yawed and fell from down the slope as someone moved back and forth in a search pattern. Motorbikes or ATVs.

Spurred by the sounds, Jessie snatched a pair of saddles by the pommels and swung them up on the horses' backs. Merry was placing a blanket on Bravo. Sandy was alert but unmoving. She knelt on the ground sheet they shared, her hands shaking, her loose hair hiding her face.

Levon took Sandy's arm in a firm, even grip and helped her to her feet. Her eyes met his. They were red rimmed and wet. Her chin quivered though her arm was warm through the flannel sleeve.

"The men that were going to hurt you? They're dead. The men coming for us now? They'll be dead soon. Do you believe me, honey?"

She nodded, sniffing.

"Now do what your mother says and it's all going to be all right. Can you do that?"

"Yes," she said. A small voice.

"Yes, what?"

"Yes, sir," she said. Louder, more sure, this time.

"You'll do fine, honey." Levon laid a gentle hand on her face. He turned to Jessie.

"Walk the horses up to the crest. Over the lee of the hill you'll find a hunt trail running along the ridge. Turn right on it. It'll take you down to Mosby Creek. Follow the creek to where it runs under the county road where the Mason lodge is."

"I know the place," Jessie said.

"Wait for me in the woods above the lodge. Take my horse along with you."

"How will you catch up? You'll be on foot," Jessie said.

"Not for long," he said.

The buzzsaw roar of an ATV rose through the trees from below.

Gunny Leffertz said:
> *"Stick and move. Stick and move. Never be where they think you are. Always be where they think you ain't."*

48

He followed the man and machine over the front post of the carbine. The guy was leaning on the handlebars, standing crouched, to keep his weight forward as he climbed the grade. An automatic rifle was bungied across the fork. The shaved head swiveled left and right as he rode.

The first slug took him in the chest. The rider struggled to control the ATV. It wavered and swerved until it was perpendicular to the grade. The driver's weight pulled it over sideways to capsize hard into the pine needles, tumbling over once. The motor died with a cough. The weight of it rolled over the rider. He let out a yelp like a wounded dog.

Levon was on the move as the machine continued toppling into the trees below. Carbine up and advancing in a sideways gait to maintain his footing. The needle floor of the forest was slick with dew.

The man was still alive and struggling. The .44 mag had punched a wicked keyhole wound into his lung. The lips of the wound moved as wind sucked in through the opening. The weight of the ATV left his hips crushed. A tip of white bone stuck through the leg of his jeans where a thigh had snapped, tearing through flesh and fabric. He was a young man. His face was turning blue as he starved for air. His mouth was open in a perpetual gasp. His eyes fought to stay focused. It was a losing battle.

Levon kept his ears attuned to the forest below. More engine sounds converged, trying to find the source of the single rifle shot. He crouched by the dying man and searched the pockets of his jeans. The man moaned deep in his throat, a palsied hand reaching for Levon's arm. He had the head of a snarling wolf tattooed on his chest below curved letters spelling out "Lupo."

Levon found keys, a crushed pack of cigarettes and a cell phone. He pocketed the phone after wiping blood from it. He tossed the ring of keys far into the woods.

The man was dead by the time Levon stepped over him to move at an angle down the hill to meet the mechanical sounds growing louder. He took up a position behind the thick bole of a mature spruce. Below him a dark shape flashed between the trees. Another ATV. It was on a path to climb the slope at an oblique angle. He waited, watching as the man and machine returned in the opposite direction, closer now. The searchers were using a crisscross pattern to hunt for their comrade and the source of the rifle shot. Another ATV motor could be heard, but not seen, farther to Levon's left.

No cell footprint out here. They might believe that the rifle shot was their friend signaling them. Levon knelt low and braced the carbine against the bark of the tree. In his peripheral he saw the dark shape returning from off to his right. He took in a breath, let it out slow, and trained the sights on a gap between the trees in the path of the returning ATV. It came into his field of vision fifty yards beneath him, coming on at a steep angle. He gave the rider a half second's lead and pressed the trigger home.

The slug took the rider through his helmeted head. The rider, limp as though made of rags, slid from the saddle. The machine puttered to a stop, upright, on the slope. The second machine was closing on a direct path, following the echoes of the carbine's big boom echoing down the hillside.

Levon ran full out on a slant to his left, running and sliding down the incline to meet the third machine. He dropped behind a tree, his back braced to it. The machine drew closer, charging straight up the slope, engine screaming. The ATV passed his position to his left, the rider standing on the frame. His head turning as he rode, scanning the woods above.

Two shots to the back, a double tap. Levon held the carbine snug to his shoulder to jack the lever again and again. The rider pitched over the handlebars to roll back down the way he came. The ATV choked and barked and came to rest canted sideways on the slope.

Levon ran to the man lying face down in the needles. The two holes in the back of his t-shirt were only inches apart. Either one was lethal. The man lay still as only the dead can. Levon searched his pockets. Another pack of cigarettes. A lighter. A fold of cash secured in a gold clip decorated with a human skull. And a cell phone. He took the lighter, cash and phone.

An electronic quack and hiss came from the ATV, its engine ticking as it cooled. Levon found a walkie talkie secured in a sleeve on the handlebars. He keyed the send button twice. A voice asked questions in Spanish. It called out names. Lupo. Munez. Jorgito. The speaker sounded breathless. There were traces of voices in the background. Men complaining. Levon held the radio away from his face and pressed the send button.

"Where are you? We have him now," Levon said in Spanish.

"Is he alive?" the voice on the walkie demanded.

"*Sí.*"

"Keep him alive. It will take us time to reach you."

"*Sí.* We will."

"Who is this? Lupo?"

Levon snapped the radio off and clipped it to his belt.

There were more of them. On foot. They were coming.

Levon would wait.

49

El Chistoso sat with the windows of the Audi rolled down in order to smell the morning air.

A cold wind dropped down through the trees above to wash over the grounds of the horse ranch. It carried with it the heady scent of pine sap. It reminded him of winters spent on his grandfather's farm, a plot of dirt two acres square, high in the hills above Galeana. There were horses there, too. They belonged to a neighboring *estancia*, a place with hundreds of acres owned by a wealthy oil man. He would visit that man's villa sometimes with his grandfather.

The two men would talk on the shaded veranda, one a powerful Pemex executive, the other a humble *campesino*. But while they shared mescal from a clay jug they were equals. *Mexicanos*.

He would spend his time there in the stables, overcome with a child's wonder at all the horses in their many breeds. To him, the stable was like a palace. It was much finer than the shack he lived in with his parents and siblings. Stalls of oak with gleaming steel bars. A floor of fitted slate. High ceilings with fans hanging beneath, stirring the air with huge wicker blades. And the scent of straw and manure. To him it did not smell of shit. To him it was a sweet odor, earthy. It was an odor that told him that all things were possible in this life. Even for a horse to live better than a man.

El Chistoso filled his nose with the sweet tang of the stalls coming from the open stable doors. The others told him that a horse lay dead inside. That touched him with sadness. A sadness not visible on the frozen features of his ravaged face. A sadness he did not feel for the men lying dead here. They were stupid, vain, *gabachos*. He would not mourn for them.

Nor would he mourn the man being hunted through the trees above. But that man he could respect. He looked forward to meeting the man. He looked forward to punishing the man. He looked forward to, once he had wrung all the pain he could from the man's body, putting a bullet in the man's brain.

Carlos stood outside the car, listening for the sounds of the machines. Those sounds were lost to him by distance now. He listened for the machines' return. He heard the brittle crack of rifle fire far away. But that was nothing unusual in these woods. It could be anything.

The phone in his pocket vibrated. It was Lupo.

"Where are you?" he said.

"Are you in charge?" Fluent Spanish spoken in a flat tone. Without accent.

"Who is this?"

"If you were in charge you would know who this is," the voice said. No inflection.

"I will let you talk to him," Carlos said. He trotted to the Audi.

"Yes? You have something for me?" Chistoso said.

"*La Yegua.*" It was the gringo. He spoke Spanish well but still with a *yanqui* accent.

What did he mean by *la yegua*? The mare. Like the horse shot dead in the stable stall.

"What are you saying?"

"You have been there?"

"*Ai.* I have been there," Chistoso said. Not a horse but a place. A long spit of sand off the Gulf coast of Mexico. Broad sand beaches and salt marshes.

"You weren't there seven years ago."

Chistoso said nothing. His features darkened.

"Good Friday."

Chistoso's eyes folded into black slits.

"Monte Lugo," the gringo said. "Roberto Salazar. Nino Raza."

"They are all dead," Chistoso said.

Carlos looked into the Audi to see the old man's hands clench. The road map of ancient scars across his knuckles turned white.

"You are only alive because you were not there that night."

"You know me, *yanqui*?"

"I know of you. One of your men told me you were here before he died."

"And *La Yegua*. How do you know of that?"

"I was there that night."

"How can I believe you, *yanqui*?"

"I told you the names. Do you need more? Humberto Sosa. Antonio Ruiz. Tiki Ramos."

Chistoso shouted, "How do you know these names?"

Carlos stepped away from the Audi, eyes on the old man foaming at the voice on the other end of the line.

"I was there."

Chistoso said nothing. He sat back in the plush seat. His shoulders dropped under the full weight of his years. He recalled *La Yegua* and the day seven years before. He was to be there but for the weather grounding his plane in Vera Cruz. He remembered the funerals, the widows crying. The coffins empty because the bodies of the men were never found. Their deaths a mystery, a deep secret known only to the *patróns* of the Zetas crew.

"They are all dead, Martin Aguilar."

The old man nodded.

"Do you understand?"

"I understand."

The connection broke. Chistoso tossed the dead phone atop the dash.

"Get in and drive," he said to Carlos.

"Where? The others have not returned," Carlos said. He stared, witness to the man aging twenty years before his eyes.

"They will not be returning. Now drive."

50

His phone rang and rang, jittering across the bedside table like an angry insect. He turned up the volume on the cheapjack motel TV. A game show with that guy who used to be fat joking and laughing with some woman who was currently fat.

Merle Hogue had no intention of picking up. It would be his cousin up in Missouri looking for news, an update. Merle had nothing promising for him. And Lou Bragg wasn't a man to take bad news with a cool head. Or worse, maybe Lou had gotten wind of the total buttfuck this situation in Alabama had become and was looking to chew him a brand new asshole.

He hadn't heard from Roy Mathers since late in the afternoon the day before. Same for Granger and Gary Bush. They went out looking for this half-brother of the ex-deputy and stepped off the face of the planet. How was he to explain a thing like that to Lou? Besides, his cousin's most likely response would be to send him, Merle Hogue, after those old boys. And Merle did not fancy that, no sir. He wasn't the least bit curious to find out where those old boys got to. And even less eager to join them.

The Mexes had not called either. Merle was not certain whether to take that as a good sign or not. Could mean anything. No one knew what got into the mind of a greaser. Maybe they'd already packed up and headed back over the border. One thing was certain, he had no desire to ever meet up with the owner of that voice on the other end of the phone. The one calling the shots in the background, telling the younger greaser what to say. The man sounded like he gargled Drano. Like he was speaking from the bottom of a grave.

He had a number written on a motel notepad. One of the Mathers' crew assigned to drive him around while he was down here in the sticks. Young kid with a crewcut and bad teeth. He dialed the number. The boy picked up, voice sullen with sleep.

"You sober, boy?" Merle said.

"Sure am. This Mister Hogue?"

"Damn right. I need you to come round here to the Roadway Motel, place you dropped me off yesterday."

"How soon?" the boy said. Merle could hear a female voice drawling in the background. Drowsy and asking questions.

"Now, damn it," Merle said. He hung up.

He went to the closet and pulled out his overnight bag. He plucked his suit bag off the hanging bar and laid it flat on the bed. He'd have the kid drive him to the municipal airport and hop a flight back to St. Louis. If it was to be bad news Merle decided it would be best to deliver it in person. Less likely Lou would send him after the missing men. More likely Lou would send some of his guys more accustomed to the rough work. Merle thought of himself as more of a fixer than a fighter. He knew his cousin thought of him as an errand boy.

Packed up, he humped the bags out of the room and onto the lot. The kid was already there, the engine of his piece-of-shit Charger running. Merle walked out to meet him. The boy—was it Tripp? Trap? Troy?—stayed behind the wheel, not even getting out to help.

"Pop the fucking trunk," Merle barked. He slammed the flat of his hand onto the lid.

A metallic click and the trunk sprung open. The kid was in the trunk. Travis? Squeezed in with his knees up against his chest. His spiky haircut matted with drying blood. Merle looked up over the trunk lid. Some Mex with a dark face grinned at him over the seat back from behind the wheel.

Merle moved to turn, dropping his bags. A sharp pain made

him see white. He saw the ground rise to meet him, his own reflection in the chrome of the bumper staring back at him with a lost expression.

It was cold when he woke up. Hurt like the devil when he opened his eyes. He raised his head and regretted it. His cheek was tacky with drying vomit. A gag rose up his throat to end as a dry wretch.

"*El está despierto.*" A voice behind him.

Merle rolled over onto his back. Above him was the curved roof of a metal shed powdered with rust. He realized with a sickening start that he was naked.

A face came into view. At first Merle thought the man wore a mask. It was a face not fully formed. Like a sculptor had stopped halfway. Deeply scored with pits and scars and patches of discolored flesh. The mouth a lipless slit. The eyes bored into him from deep craters of ravaged tissue.

"*Ayudarle a levantarse, Carlito*," the man with the dead face said.

Another face loomed above. The Mex he'd seen behind the wheel of the Charger. He lifted Merle first to a sitting position and then to his feet. Merle's vision spun. The shed jiggled back and forth before his eyes. His throat contracted. He felt the urge to puke. Nothing came up.

The young man, Carlito, helped him walk to the center of the shed. A Quonset hut, Merle realized through the dull haze wrapped about his head like a blanket. There were probably hundreds of these government surplus shacks in these hills. Lots of hoopies used them to house stills back in the day.

Two barrels sat upright on the concrete floor. Steel barrels.

Fifty gallons. One open. One sealed. A concrete block sat next to the sealed one. There was an orange box, cable and a gun sort of tool on a rolling metal cart. Merle recognized it as a spot welder.

As they stumbled closer, Merle saw fresh welds around the circumference of the sealed barrel's lid. There was the scent of hot metal in the air.

The man with the dead face stooped to pick up the cinder block and move it next to the empty barrel.

"*Entra en el barril,*" the man with the dead face said.

"Get in the barrel," the younger man said.

A sound was coming from inside the sealed barrel. A muffled shriek punctuated by feeble rapping on the interior of the steel shell.

Merle blinked, fighting to remain lucid, as the younger man helped him step up onto the cinder block. The younger man held Merle's arm to help him keep balance while he placed first one leg and then the other inside the drum. Gentle pressure applied to his head made him squat deeper, deeper, until his hair line was below the lip of the barrel.

It all seemed like he was watching it from far away. Or on a movie screen. He scrunched his neck and canted his head painfully to look up. The opening was eclipsed by the barrel lid being fitted in place, leaving him in darkness. He winced as a rubber mallet banged atop the lid to set it firmly in place. The impacts echoed inside the barrel, sounding like rifle shots.

Now all was total dark. He strained his eyes wider. Only blackness through white lace. His only company was his own shallow breathing. A pop and hiss from outside. A wave of warm air washed down from above. The barrel filled with the oily smell of scorched steel. The heat turned from a pleasant glow to a furnace heat within seconds.

The change brought him back to his senses as the hiss and pop continued and the interior of the barrel became a sweltering oven.

And then he screamed and screamed and screamed.

51

Some kids, a pair of brothers, found a tricked out ATV under the shadows of the iron bridge that ran over Mosby Creek. They kept it hidden for a few days in the woods behind the Mason lodge. Their father caught them sneaking a can of gas out to it. He took it away from his sons and sold it on to a guy he knew down in Randolph County. Dad got eight hundred bucks cash. It was gone to Jim Beam, cigarettes and lottery scratchers inside of a week.

Two counties over, the body of a man, a white male, was found by hikers up from Samford University. They were communing with nature for a week before school restarted. Rather, they put up tents and got stoned out of their minds far from the prying eyes of parents and police. One of them left the giggling company to take "a wicked shit" and stumbled across the remains of a white male, stripped of his clothes and covered with bugs.

They argued for a day and half over whether to do their civic duty and report their find or just say "fuck it" and head back to school. They gave themselves a day of abstinence to transform back into sober, dedicated pre-law students before calling 911. Their clothes still reeked of cannabis when the deputies arrived. The cops paid no heed. The stinking corpse lying naked in a copse of cottonwoods was enough of a paperwork headache.

The torso, face and legs showed signs of a severe beating with a blunt object or objects. Broken ribs, two broken legs. Animals, coons or wild dogs, had been at the face, buttocks and guts. Wild dogs most likely. That was the opinion of the deputies who knew from experience that dogs and coyotes started at the ass end of their kills. Raccoons were the culprit for the missing face.

The corpse's hands had been severed. The hands remained missing despite a meticulous search for them in the surrounding woods. The cuts were the work of some kind of power tool. A reciprocating saw was the ME's guess. He was certain the amputations were post-mortem. Not so the removal of every one of the victim's teeth. The man had been alive for all of that. Bits of root still clung to the gums. The ME's theory was the teeth were knocked out using a hammer and a chisel or even a flathead screwdriver.

The body was destined to be a John Doe for the time being. That changed when the ME performed a full autopsy and found a pair of teeth in the man's stomach. Third molar upper. First molar lower. The victim swallowed them during the beating he'd received.

It was more than a week before the teeth came back as a match from records at a dental clinic up in Haley.

James Mitchell "Dale" Cade.

It wouldn't be till spring that some boys playing hooky from the high school found two cars at the bottom of the quarry lake off Murdoch Road.

A Mercedes SUV and an El Camino sitting side by side in the deep green water as natural as if they were parked on the lot outside Walmart.

Things slowed to a crawl then a full stop in Danny Huff's investigation.

Mass killings, fires, and random homicides of white males and Hispanic males fell off dramatically in the county. Concurrent with the cessation of incidents of violent crime was the evaporation of witnesses, persons of interest and any other parties who might have information useful to state CID.

"I think we took our last spin of the wheel, Ralph," Danny said.

They sat in a booth at Fay's watching a man pilot a combine down what served as the main street of Colby. A dark man sat up in the air-conditioned cab. He wore a t-shirt with the flag of Mexico printed front and back. A Copenhagen gimme cap worn backwards on his head. It chugged by slow with kids and old men standing on the sidewalk watching it pass.

"We gave it a shot, sir," Trooper Durward said. He could see his own reflection in the glass and decided it was time for a haircut.

"What shot? We missed. Missed our chance to know just exactly what the fuck was going on around here. Missed by a long country mile."

"What's there to do? Every witness that might have been of use is unavailable."

Danny barked and snuffled. He lifted his mug to his lips.

"You mean dead, missing or some other damned thing. Near's I can calculate, your local bad boys, the Mathers and their ilk, tangled with some kind of cartel bunch. They had at it. Bunch of Mexican nationals turn up dead all over the landscape. As for the Mathers clan? They are gone as if taken by the rapture leaving us nothing but trailers full of widows and orphans who wouldn't tell us what day it is if it was Christmas morning. And besides, they don't know shit-all anyway."

"It is the damnedest thing," Trooper Durward said.

"And it's going to have to stay that way. I'm leaving for Mobile. That murder suicide thing? You see that on the news? The guy offed his mom and his wife and went down to the Winn-Dixie to raise more hell until the store manager blew his head off with a twenty gauge."

"Mobile. At least you might get to see the ocean."

"Might. Probably not."

"It was an honor working with you, sir," Trooper Durward said.

"Same here, man. Sorry this whole thing turned to a dry hole on us," Danny Huff said.

They turned their eyes back to the combine. It lumbered away to the edge of town with a wake of kids on bikes following after. A pair of barking dogs ran with the kids until the big John Deere picked up speed and vanished into the distance.

52

"I can do this myself," Merry said. She was on tiptoes in her wellies, brushing Bravo's long black mane smooth.

"No trouble," Uncle Fern said. He was filling the water bucket with a hose stuck through the stall posts. The ridgeback lay atop a stack of hay bales, pale eyes taking in everything.

"But I promised I'd do all the work myself," she said.

"Well I notice you were nowhere to be found when your daddy and me gutted the barn and put these stalls in," he said. He was smiling.

"I *wanted* to help."

"Yes you did, honey. But all's you were doing was getting in the way."

He leaned on the top of the stall wall to watch his niece brush the bay gelding's withers free of dust. She sprayed Bravo's legs and tail with fly repellent.

"You think Daddy will get a horse?" she said.

"I do not. Horses are a frivolous thing and your father is not a frivolous man."

"What about me? Why do I get to have Bravo then?"

"Because a girl needs her frivols. If that's a word. When Levon gets back he and I'll put in a regular tack room."

"You don't need to do all that for me. I can hang my stuff on the wall," she said.

"Saddles and traps need to be out of the damp and dust," he said.

"And the new concrete floor down the center aisle. That was a lot of trouble to go to," Merry said.

He looked down at the fresh concrete walk he and his nephew poured the previous weekend. Four by four squares in a row down the center of the barn floor. The concrete was a foot thick and covered six feet of fresh clean fill.

"That was just something needed to be done," Fern said.

"We need to get a goat," Merry said. It was an announcement that broke Fern away from his thoughts.

"A goat?"

"To keep Bravo company. We don't want him to be out here all alone, do we?" Merry said. A final loving pat between the horse's ears. She stepped out into the aisle to swing the stall door closed and secure the latch in place, the horse in for the night.

"We sure don't," Fern said. He walked with her to the house past the empty car port and into the house for dinner.

Gunny Leffertz said:
> *"Never leave a friend behind. Never leave an enemy alive."*

53

It was Wednesday.

Hump Day, Lou Bragg thought to himself with a dry chuckle. That little joke of his never got stale.

He steered the Lincoln to back into the space, the license plate facing the wall of the garage. He climbed the stairs to the second floor, a tad out of breath as he arrived at the company condo. He unlocked the door with a card key of which there were only two copies.

Lou called Carlotta's name. No answer. No smells from the kitchen either. She usually had take-out for him on Wednesdays. She reheated it in the oven in her own Pyrex dishes and made like she cooked it herself. He knew better but let her enjoy that little fiction. Lou wasn't here for the girl's cooking.

He cruised through the kitchen. Breakfast dishes still on the counter. She hadn't been back here since she left for work. Not like her. She was usually here well before him on Wednesdays, showered and wearing something he bought for her.

Carlotta Poteet was miles away in the lot of an Olive Garden where all four tires of her company leased car had been slashed flat. She was speaking to a pair of understanding policemen who were filling out a report that she could turn into Gateway Realty and Title's insurance provider. A tow truck was on the way.

Lou Bragg had no idea about that. He got a glass from the cupboard and loaded it with ice. A bit of spring water from a bottle. A jigger, maybe two, of Maker's Mark splashed on top. He made for the living room to kill time waiting in front of the TV.

A man stood in the living room before the drawn shades. He stood with a nasty looking automatic held in hands covered in blue surgical gloves. The automatic was trained on Lou's head. The gun was a big bore but looked like a toy in the man's large hands.

Lou's gaze went from the staring black eye of the .45 to the place where the big screen used to hang on the wall. In its place was a square ragged hole cut in the wall. In the middle of the room, in a mess of plaster dust, lay the safe that once filled the space behind the Sony. The rear wall of the safe had been peeled back. A power tool lay on the deep pile carpet. A thick orange cord ran to an extension on the wall. Packets of banded bills were stacked on the leather sectional. Other papers lay scattered about the room.

"Look, we can work out whatever this is," Lou Bragg said.

He wore his negotiator smile, the one that brought him up from errand boy in the Dixie mafia to one of its Big Men in the inner circle.

The smile was still fixed on his face when Carlotta found him lying on the broadloom with a single purple hole in his forehead.

Carlotta sighed and tabbed 911. She hoped the cops who answered this call were as cute as the pair who helped her back at the Olive Garden.

54

"Julian Hernandez, my dimpled ass. He doesn't look any kind of Cuban to me."

"And his Spanish sounds like he learned it from George Bush."

A Miami-Dade detective lieutenant and a DEA agent stood looking through the one-way glass at a sad-looking older man seated at a table in the interrogation room. The man, according to himself, was one Dr. Julian Luis Hernandez. He was dressed in a polo shirt and khakis. They hung off him, a sign of recent weight loss. His skin was tanned to a mahogany that set off his crown of white hair and ivory brows. A fringe of white goatee was around his downturned mouth.

"What's his story? What's my agency's interest here?" the DEA agent said.

"We had sixteen deaths from counterfeit oxy in the county over the weekend. Pills looked like the real thing. But they were loaded up with fentanyl," the detective said.

"Some asshole compounded them wrong. Our faux Cubano here?"

"No. He just sells them. Has a pill mill in Plantation. Has some kind of doctor's credentials whipped up. We're checking on it. Writes scrips for the real thing. But just started direct selling the phony oxy."

"Any ideas on his supplier?"

"A Jake outfit. The pill mill's on their turf. The doc is not being helpful."

"You want me to talk to him?" the DEA agent said.

"When his prints get back. We'll know more then. Shouldn't be a minute or so," the detective said.

They small talked a while. Both looked forward to cooler

weather coming next month. Neither looked forward to the increased local drug traffic as the snowbirds arrived. As they talked, the man at the table drooped to rest his head on folded hands. He appeared to have fallen asleep.

A clerk arrived with a sheaf of fresh faxes. The detective and DEA agent shared them, reading them over in silence. There were fingerprints on file. A three page report from the Alabama state CID. Typed single space. A printout for a BOLO from the FBI and a printed-out email from Treasury.

"Damn," the detective said.

"This guy murdered his wife up in Alabama," the DEA agent said.

"And that's just for starters. There's a hold order from Treasury. What do you want to do?"

"Go to lunch?" The DEA agent shrugged.

"Bye-bye, jerk-off," the detective said. He rapped on the glass, startling the man inside awake, eyes blinking.

The man who was still insisting he was Dr. Julian Hernandez, in clumsy Spanish straight out of Rosetta Stone, was spending his second day in a two-man cell in county. There were currently six men in the cell awaiting trial. Dr. Hernandez spent a sleepless night on the cold concrete floor.

When he did doze off, for what felt like seconds at a time, he'd be shocked awake by the noises around him. The other men in the cells seemed to never sleep. They argued, sang, coughed, farted and laughed. He awoke one time to find himself looking up into the face of a man in dreadlocks seated on the steel toilet defecating noisily into the bowl inches from his head. The man fixed him in a gaze of pure contempt, eyebrows beetled and nose wrinkled. The cell filled with an invisible cloud of beefy vapor.

When the deputy called his name, his real name, from the cell door he sprang up. He was eager to be taken anywhere that meant he could leave this tiny room filled with smelly, dangerous men.

He was cuffed and led from the cell area to a windowless room two floors below. The cuffs were secured through a ring bolt set in a heavy table. The deputy left him alone to look at himself in the wide mirrored pane set in one wall of the room.

He barely recognized himself. His face was creased with wrinkles from days in the sun. His head seemed large atop a neck thinner than he recalled. The goatee needed trimming. His eyes sunk deep into his face, lids heavy. The black and white striped jumpsuit hung off his narrow shoulders. He looked like a pantomime of a chain gang convict. What a barbaric place Florida was.

There would be someone or several someones watching him through the glass. They knew who he was now. But what did they see? What did he look like to them? A fallen man? An unredeemable criminal? Or did they see him as he saw himself, a man out of place in circumstances not of his own making. A man who, with all other options taken from him, chose the easiest path.

There was a knock at the door, a pretense at civility. The door swung inward. A man entered. Tall in a dark suit, a laminated ID card swinging from his neck on a lanyard. His suit smelled of a hint of cigarette smoke. He had the dark eyes of a predator. He took the seat opposite the doctor and set a digital recording device between them.

"Anthony Marcoon. United States Treasury. Interviewing Dr. Jordan Roth. The time is two-fifteen p.m. on October twenty-fourth."

"Is this about my wife?" Dr. Jordan Roth said.

The tall man's eyes glittered for an instant.

"Part of it. Mostly I want to talk to you about your son-in-law. Levon Cade."

Chuck Dixon is the prolific author of thousands of comic book scripts for *Batman and Robin, the Punisher, Nightwing, Conan the Barbarian, Airboy, the Simpsons, Alien Legion* and countless other titles.

Together with Graham Nolan, Chuck created the now iconic Batman villain Bane. He also wrote the international bestselling graphic novel adaptation of J.R.R.Tolkien's *The Hobbit*.

He currently writes two series for Bruno Books: the time travel epic Bad Times, as well as the ebook sensation Levon Cade. His zombie apocalypse novel *Gomers* is set to start production as a feature film in the fall of 2016. He also adapted Peter Schweitzer's controversial bestseller *Clinton Cash* into a graphic novel.

He calls Florida home these days.

Visit the Dixonverse!
(dixonverse.blogspot.com)

Made in the USA
Columbia, SC
02 February 2018